-Adventures of Bud Thompson-

Creatures of the Lake

R. E. Rowe

iUniverse, Inc.
Bloomington

Creatures of the Lake

Copyright © 2011 R. E. Rowe

*This is a work of fiction. All of the characters, names, incidents,
organizations, and dialogue in this novel are either the products
of the author's imagination or are used fictitiously.*

iUniverse books may be ordered through booksellers or by contacting:

iUniverse
1663 Liberty Drive
Bloomington, IN 47403
www.iuniverse.com
1-800-Authors (1-800-288-4677)

ISBN: 978-1-4620-1127-8 (pbk)
ISBN: 978-1-4620-1126-1 (ebk)

Library of Congress Control Number: 2011905448

Printed in the United States of America

iUniverse rev. date: 5/3/11

To Angelica, Sienna, Lexi, and Sydney Ella:
Reach for the stars,
where
the fuel of passion burns
and ideas go
supernova.

Acknowledgments

Thanks to all of those who made suggestions as earlier versions of the manuscript evolved and the current one was finalized: technical guru, sci-fi fan, and good friend David Olynick, PhD; publicist and editor Carol Hoenig; editor Elizabeth Day; and my wonderful wife, Michelle, for her continued support, encouragement, and love. Thanks also to my family, my friends, and fellow geeks who share my belief that education, science, inventing, and innovation can be incredibly fun, surprisingly cool, and the path to an exciting future.

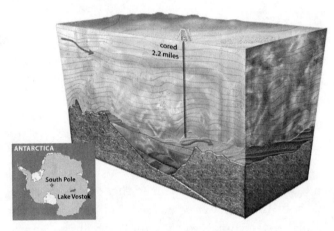

Zina Deretsky / NSF

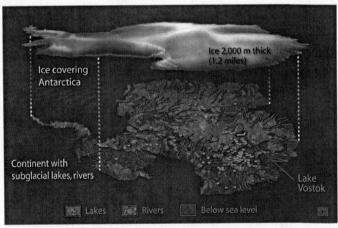

Image credit: Nicolle Rager-Fuller / NSF

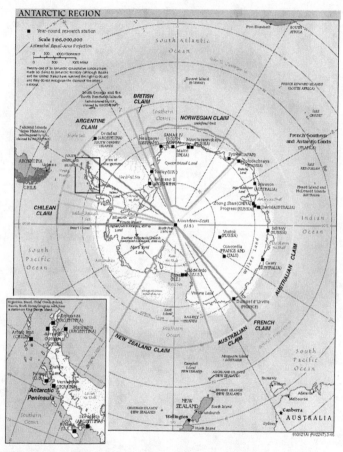

Original Map produced by Central Intelligence Agency
http://www.nsf.gov/news/news_images.
jsp?cntn_id=109587&org=ANT

— I —

BUD MADE A COUPLE of minor adjustments to his electronic device before connecting the small battery. A red light blinked twice and then glowed bright green as Bud quickly sealed the device in a small, folded white envelope and brought his attention back to boring Ms. Ferguson.

Even though he was in his freshman year of high school, the class work was no challenge for Bud. The only challenge was keeping his mind on prepositions and verbs rather than his latest invention.

"… in order to get full credit for the assignment," said Ms. Ferguson as she turned her back to the class to write the assignment on the chalkboard, "your report must be twelve pages, double spaced." The class sighed as she paused before continuing to write on the blackboard. "The report is due in one week."

Bud kept his eye on Ted James, an oversized goon towering over most kids in school. Ted should have been in his senior year, but had failed the last two years— no wonder, since he spent most of his time tormenting classmates and playing tabletop football in detention. This time, Ted's victim was Little Sammy, seated just in front of him. Each time Ted flicked Sammy's ear and Sammy opened his mouth to protest, Ted would poke Sammy hard in the back as a warning not to alert Ms. Ferguson.

With her back still to the class, Ms. Ferguson said sternly, "Mr. James, are you writing down the assignment?"

Ted James just looked around the classroom smugly as he made a face and rolled his eyes.

All the kids in the class, except for Bud, just looked down as Ted took another flick at Little Sammy's ear. Bud focused on Ted intensely; it was almost time.

Finally, the bell rang and Bud collected his books and his backpack in one swift move, watching Sammy escape from Ted's outreached arm and dash out of the room, pushing his way past everyone.

"Now, don't forget, class, your report is due in one week," Ms. Ferguson said loudly over the noise of screeching chairs and chatter.

Bud saw his opportunity as Ted wiggled his large body out of the desk chair and started to march toward the door. Bud smoothly maneuvered between students and casually bumped into the goon.

"Watch it, dweeb!" Ted said, pushing past Bud without noticing the small envelope that Bud slipped into his shirt pocket.

Bud trailed behind, making his way to the lockers, where his only close friend, Gregory McCallister, the tall and skinny math club president and star of the chess club, stood waiting in anticipation. His thick, dark-rimmed glasses perched awkwardly on his nose.

Popularity at school was something most kids wanted, while intelligence just wasn't a priority. In fact, being a smart kid at school usually meant becoming the target of bullies like Ted James, who felt the need to pick on the smart kids.

Bud didn't care about being popular. He had a small build with a face on the round side. His shoulder-length, thick, sandy-blond hair covered his ears and swept across his forehead, often falling down over his large, blue eyes before being moved aside by a slight jerk of his head or brush of his fingertips. Bud kept to himself most of the time and cared mostly about dreaming up cool inventions like those of his heroes: Edison, Tesla, Ford, and … well, his workaholic father.

Bud also cared about stopping bullies like Ted James from picking on smart classmates like Little Sammy. He remembered his mother telling him years ago to always stand up for what he believed in. Bud took her words to heart and wasn't about to ignore Ted's cruel behavior. It just wasn't right, and it needed to stop—now.

Bud watched Ted make his way through the crowded hallway, finally reaching Sammy at his locker. He pushed Little Sammy hard in the back.

"You ready?" asked Gregory.

Bud nodded with fire in his eyes, pulled out another electronic device from his backpack, and pushed a black button. The light on the remote control turned bright green. He pushed another button, and a second light below the handwritten word "connected" changed from bright red to bright green.

"Showtime," whispered Bud as he squinted to see Ted hovering over a cowering Sammy.

"Give me your lunch, punk," demanded Ted, expanding his oversized chest and holding Sammy's locker door open.

Bud watched as Sammy started to hand Ted the paper sack with his lunch in it. Suddenly the small boy stopped and stared at Ted, along with the other kids around him in the hallway.

Ted's face turned a purplish red as he grew angrier at the sight of the snickering kids around him. He shoved his victim a second time.

"Punk, did you hear m—"

The laughter in the hallway grew louder; now the entire hallway was filled with kids who were pointing at Ted, their whispers growing louder.

"Hey! Your lunch—"

Ted stopped, apparently realizing what everyone was hearing. Every word Ted said was being amplified and broadcast over the school's intercom, blaring out of the loudspeakers.

Tall, thin Principal Seeback (who, it was rumored, could see from the back of his head) did not appear amused as he walked down the hallway. His thin, black tie fluttered and his gray suit jacket flopped around wildly with each step he took. Mr. Rooter, the weight-lifting school janitor, struggled to keep up with Mr. Seeback as Mr. Rooter's key collection clanked loudly on his belt.

As the two men approached Ted, Mr. Seeback pointed toward Ted in a striking motion, shaking his long, bony finger, and said, "Mr. James, to my office—now!"

In a single motion and without breaking stride, Mr. Rooter grabbed Ted by the collar with one rippling arm. He pulled hard, dragging Ted in the direction of Mr. Seeback's office as if the boy were a mere twenty-five-pound dumbbell.

Little Sammy didn't look so little anymore. He stood tall and smiled now that the pea-brained goon was firmly in Mr. Rooter's grasp.

Bud gave him the thumbs-up as students throughout the hallway clapped, ignoring Ted's attempted threat as Ted waved a fist at them.

Mr. Rooter gave Ted's collar a sharp jerk, causing Ted's fist to open and his arm to go limp.

Without so much as a glance backward, Principal Seeback shouted, "Show's over, people. Now get to class!"

Gregory laughed. "Wicked cool, dude," he told Bud. "You totally rock! Meet you at your tree house later?"

Bud smiled, nodded, and then put his backpack on and dashed down the hallway as Gregory went in the opposite direction.

2

THE WOODEN TREE HOUSE had been built firmly into the old sprawling oak tree towering two stories above Bud's spacious backyard. The twisted, thick branches pointed in all directions, with patches of leaves providing touches of privacy here and there. Bud and Gregory sat comfortably as they surveyed the surrounding area in two old, beaten-up stuffed leather chairs Bud had found in front of his neighbor's house one trash day.

Casey, a small mixed-breed mutt with large brown eyes, long ears, sat comfortably in Bud's lap, drooling down Bud's blue jeans and onto his worn high-top sneakers. Bud's father had found Casey in the animal shelter ten years earlier. Casey was getting on in years and hobbled around like a ninety-eight-year-old man, bumping into walls and furniture due to his limited eyesight. Of course, his hearing was no better, and oftentimes caused quite a bit of concern when he became excited and wandered off, as he was known to do from time to time. His short, floppy tail, however, hadn't lost its wildly energetic wag.

Sara sat below them, outside of Bud's nearby house, in a crouching position, trying to muffle her sobbing.

Her long, blonde hair covered most of her slim face and flowed over her shoulders, reaching the porch step. She wiped the tears from her face as fast as they ran down her cheeks. What little makeup she wore was running down her cheeks in streaks.

Gregory peered down. "What's wrong with your sister?"

"Ah, she broke up with her boyfriend or something," Bud said, trying to downplay the real reason she was crying.

"You mean with the football star, Tony—Tony Campbell?"

"Yeah, I think he's the guy," Bud said.

There was a long pause. Gregory's face transitioned from sincere concern into a mischievous teenage grin and asked, "Think she'd go out with me?"

Bud threw a nearby leather pillow at Gregory, causing Casey to jump off his lap. "Aw, jeez!" Bud said, just as his grandmother shouted his name from the house. "I gotta go in for dinner. Let's meet up at school on Monday."

Gregory scowled. "Monday? Thought we had the whole weekend to hang, dude?"

"Nope, I'm goin' to work with my dad at the Space Center," Bud said.

"The Space Center? Way cool! Think I can—"

"Sorry, no can do," Bud said with a half grin. "My dad said security will only let family members in over the weekend." Bud had to force himself not to gloat, but at that moment, he felt cooler than he had in a long time—even cooler than when he had made a fool out of that goon Ted.

Gregory sighed and lowered Casey down in a basket tied to a rope. Finally, both boys climbed down the wooden ladder attached to the wide tree trunk.

"Later, dude," Gregory said as he jumped from the ladder and ran toward his house down the street.

At the back door of his house, Bud was greeted by the aroma of his grandmother's homemade lasagna, causing his stomach to growl in anticipation. Sara was still sitting on the back steps, her hands holding her head.

"Why you crying, anyway?" Bud asked.

Sara looked up, her face covered in tears. Casey hobbled slowly by her, stopping briefly to lick her bare knees.

"Leave me alone!" she muttered.

"Grams is worried about you," he said, scooting around her and pulling Casey's collar.

"I'm seventeen years old. She doesn't have to tell me what to do anymore," Sara said as she started sobbing again, covering her face with her hands.

Sara was still crying into the palms of her hands as Bud entered the house with Casey leading the way. He slammed the door behind him and headed straight for the dinner table in the dining room. As Bud moved with urgency through the kitchen toward the table, he barely even noticed the table was formally set with a freshly pressed tablecloth and Grams's finest china place settings. Instead, Bud focused on the salad and French bread that were already on the table as his stomach growled loudly.

The soft lines on Grams's old face deepened as her fragile frame leaned over the open oven door, carefully sliding the pan of bubbling lasagna out with her trembling hands. She had moved in with Bud's family after his mother had died nearly five years ago. Grams originally had come to stay for a couple of weeks when it happened and had been there ever since.

"I'm starving, Grams," Bud said, pulling out a chair and taking in the aroma. "Oh, man, that smells good."

"Wait, child," said Grams as she moved her shiny, silver hair away from her face and took a deep breath. "Before you sit down, please let your father know dinner is ready. And where is Sara?"

"Outside the door, crying again." Bud dashed into the living room and shouted upstairs to his father. Without waiting for a reply, he returned to the table and grabbed a piece of hot French bread.

"For goodness' sake, child, how many times do I have to tell you to please wait for everyone else?" Grams sighed loudly as she placed the lasagna on a hot plate in the middle of the table, but all Bud noticed was the bubbling cheese on the side of the clear lasagna pan.

His father appeared, walking directly to the table, still in his dress shirt and tie. "Looks great, Mother." He was a tall man with short, nicely trimmed black hair combed in place with the help of hair gel. He looked as if he had not eaten for days. He wore clothes that were pressed but a couple decades old, making him look as if he had just come out of the Apollo moon mission era through a time warp.

Bud grabbed a spoon and began to scoop up some lasagna.

"Bud!" shouted Grams. "Please, child—I asked you to wait. And why are you using the salad spoon?" She handed him a spatula. "For someone as bright as you are, young man …" she muttered.

"What's the occasion?" Bud's father asked.

"Oh, no occasion," Grams said softly. "I just thought it would be nice to sit down for dinner. With you working so late so often, it's been a while since we all sat down for a meal."

But Bud knew that wasn't the real reason, as Grams usually fixed a nice meal in memory of his mother on the day of her birthday, although no one ever admitted it.

Bud's father's cell phone rang, its big screen lighting up. Bud watched his father's eyes shift to it as he looked closely at the number on the display.

"Sorry, just real quick ... I need to take this one." Bud's father got up and walked into the living room.

"This is awesome," Bud said as he shoved the food as quickly as he could into his mouth.

"Slow down, child!" Grams said. Then, managing a half smile, she added as she disappeared into the kitchen, "Thank you ... I'm glad you like it."

Bud stuffed another bite of lasagna into his mouth and then chewed and swallowed it quickly as his father returned to the table.

Bud cleared his throat. "So, what time are we going in tomorrow, Dad?" he asked.

"You need to be up at 6:00 a.m. We need to leave the house no later than 6:45, got it?" Bud's father said. "Larry will show you around the place, while I attend meetings in the morning."

"Larry ... you mean Larry Matuso?" asked Bud. "Your group scientist? Isn't he the guy we met last year at the company picnic—the one who builds all the inventions for your space projects?"

"Yes—" Bud's father started and then stopped as Grams returned with Sara, walking her slowly toward the dining table. One of Gram's arms held Sara closely as

Sara rubbed her eyes and sniffled. Both Bud and his father looked at Sara with concern as she sat down in a huff.

Bud's father looked at Bud and continued, "Yes, Bud, he's the one."

Bud shoveled another bite of lasagna into his mouth, taking his mind off Sara and focusing on his upcoming visit to the Space Center. His eyes sparkled as he grinned and chewed the mouthful of lasagna.

3

BUD STAYED ON HIS dad's heels as they reached the security gate. Inside the window of the small, freestanding guard shack, the old-fashioned, mechanical clock read 7:25.

"Good morning, Dr. Thompson," said the slightly overweight security guard stumbling out of the wooden shack. "Didn't expect you this morning sir. I see you have some help today."

Bud noticed a half-eaten glazed doughnut on the desk inside the shack, and some of the doughnut remained on the side of the guard's mouth and tie.

"You'll need this badge, young man," said the guard. He handed Bud the badge labeled "Visitor" and gestured for him to sign the security log.

"Thanks, sir." Bud stood up straight and tall and then signed the security log. For the first time, he felt as if he were one of the scientists working for his father.

Bud had to practically run to catch up with his father, who had clearly become distracted by something on his phone as he walked. His father's strides resumed their brisk pace, revealing his determination to get to that meeting he had kept mentioning to Bud on the ride to the Space Center that morning.

The heavy metal door squeaked loudly as they entered the towering building, which reminded Bud of an airplane hangar.

"Wow," Bud muttered, doing a double take as he looked inside the building. They walked down a long hallway with no doors or windows except for the large metal door at the end.

Finally, they reached the door. His father opened it and poked in his head. "Hey, Larry," he called, "I brought you a visitor."

Bud walked through the metal door into a spacious laboratory. As Bud looked up, his stomach dropped a little as he observed the soaring height of the ceiling in amazement.

"Hey, Bud. Good to see you again," Larry said, approaching him.

Bud turned to see that his father was nowhere in sight, but that was of little concern to him. "Hi, Larry," Bud said as he shook the man's hand and looked around the huge room with the three-story ceiling.

The room was the largest Bud had ever seen. Enormous shaded windows surrounded the top half of the room near the ceiling, filling the entire space with filtered natural light. Electronic equipment was scattered throughout, with boxes overflowing with parts arranged on large workbenches and soldering irons prominently mounted on the ends of the workbenches. Chemistry stations were located sporadically around the room—some filled with bubbling liquids, some giving off clouds of steam, and some sitting empty. Other large workbenches were stacked with electronic gear; flashing, multicolored displays; and segmented displays featuring bright red, ever-changing numbers.

"It seems like ages since the last company picnic!" Larry said. Larry, who was on the husky side, wore faded jeans, a colored shirt with a pocket protector loaded with pens, and a wrinkled tie that didn't match his shirt. His salt-and-pepper hair made him look as if he had just woken up, and his mustache reached his bottom lip here and there, but his smile lit up the room.

Bud wasn't interested in small talk. He just kept looking around. "This place is way cool. It looks like a forest of technology."

"Thanks. It feels like home these days, that's for sure. Bad news, though: it turns out I'm in the same meeting with your father this morning, and as usual, I'm late ... so I will need to leave you alone for a few hours. Your father got approval for you to stay here without an escort, but you have to stay in my lab, okay?"

Bud just grunted as he continued looking around. He was comfortable being alone—although at the moment, he felt anything but alone, with all the new contraptions to see around him.

"Feel free to make yourself at home," Larry said. "You have a book or something?"

"Yeah, I have my cell phone and some games I like to play," Bud said as his eyes strained to see what was in the far end of the room.

"Good," Larry said as he collected paperwork from one of the workbenches. "Stay away from my bubbling brew over there, okay?" Larry pointed to a large glass container with glass pipes running from the top of the container to the ceiling twenty feet above. It was half filled with gurgling liquid and half filled with steam. A red and black "Danger" sign displaying the word "Hydrogen" next to a picture of a flame was mounted on the middle of the container.

Bud nodded.

Larry disappeared just as quickly as Bud had arrived, but this didn't bother Bud, who was still surveying the lab.

"Nice to see you again," Larry yelled from across the room as an afterthought, followed by the loud echo of the door latching shut.

Bud strolled around the lab. A metal ball the size of a jumbo gumball attracted Bud's attention. It sat in a basket below thirty feet of white plastic pipe that went up and down and around, forming a huge knot. Bud picked up the ball and followed the pipe up, down, around, and finally to where it began. He stood on a chair, looked at the upturned mouth of a pipe at one end of the contraption, and realized the pipe opening was just slightly larger than the metal ball.

"Hmm, interesting. So if I put the ball here and drop it …"

The ball took off quickly after it entered the pipe. A burst of air came from small holes on the side of the pipes; the ball was pushing air out of each section of pipe as it moved quickly through the pipe. Bud could almost follow the ball as it moved through the inside of the pipe just by following the sound of moving air. Suddenly the contraption made a series of different loud sounds.

"Notes … it's playing notes," mumbled Bud as the ball zoomed through the pipe.

"Dah-dah dah-dah-da-da Dah-dah dah-dah-da-da," sang the ball as it fell from a pipe into a basket on the other end of the contraption with a whoosh and then a thud.

Bud stared at the metal ball for a moment before he began to laugh. *I get it!* he thought. *It was a Lady Gaga song. Now that's funny! So it makes musical sounds, like a flute, when the ball goes through the pipe.*

Bud noticed special sections of pipe in a large bin next to a workbench close to the plastic contraption. He picked up one of the small sections and shoved the metal ball through it. The pipe section had a rubbery insert on its inside walls and a small hole on its side.

"So each of these sections of pipe makes different sounds when the ball goes through them!" Bud experimented with the different sections, figuring out what sounds they made.

Bud spotted a nearby bin of pipe sections with electronics inside them. The metal pieces were mounted securely inside each small pipe section and tied to a spring that opened and closed the pieces. He noticed a small circuit board that he recognized.

Aha! Bud thought. *These can be controlled by the same sort of wireless communication I used on Ted at school.*

Bud took out his cell phone, which had a large display screen. Bud's phone was one of his prized possessions, and he had spent hours fiddling with and modifying it to allow him to send information wirelessly to the crazy electronic devices he built in his room at home.

"I wonder if I can send it a command to open and close."

Bud noticed each piece of pipe had a unique number on it. He tapped a series of buttons on his cell phone that caused a new display to appear on its screen. He tapped the buttons again to configure the phone to communicate with each uniquely numbered piece of pipe.

After he sent a command to the pipe, he held his breath, waiting.

Wamp! The metal piece inside the plastic pipe closed shut.

"Very nice!" Bud pressed a few more buttons on his cell phone.

Wamp! The metal piece inside the plastic pipe opened.

"Oh, yeah, that's what I'm talking about. Now I can connect these together to make different sounds, and I can change the direction of the ball by opening and closing sections of pipe."

Nearly three hours later, Larry returned. Larry stood with his mouth open just past the open laboratory door and looked in amazement at the structure Bud had created with the plastic pipes. Sections of pipe wove up, down, and around into a sculpture. Bud's newly created maze of plastic tubing pathways and metal levers extended all around a large area in the lab, with pipe sections sloping like miniature roller-coaster hills or spinning as rapidly as a merry-go-round.

Bud was busy testing his invention and using his cell phone to control the route of the balls he placed in the top section of pipe. Three metal balls traveled along the plastic pathways, making music as they danced through the pipes and then fell into the basket below.

"What the—?" started Larry in a serious tone as his eyes followed the large pipe contraption Bud had created.

"Oh … hi, Larry. I guess I got a little carried away. But check this out," Bud said as he quickly placed three more metal balls, one right after the other, into the plastic contraption. Off the balls went, in a burst of air.

Suddenly loud music began to play from the giant contraption as Bud rapidly tapped the screen of his cell phone, controlling the metal balls. Three separate melodies played all at once, harmonizing with one another. Then the three metal balls fell into three separate baskets at the same time, as if sticking their landings after competing in a gymnastics vault competition: *womp!*

"I see you discovered our latest R&D project," Larry said, looking at what Bud had built. "Impressive," he added under his breath, his eyes wide. "That sounded like three Lady Gaga songs all playing at once. I think Gaga and her 'little monsters' would be impressed."

Bud smiled as his face turned red.

"You're hired as my intern," Larry said. "That work for you?"

Bud just stared wide-eyed at Larry.

"Won't pay anything," Larry added, "but you'll have the run of the place and I could use a good technician around here."

Bud vigorously nodded yes. "When do I start?"

"You already have. Now let me show you the really fun stuff we have in my technoforest, as you called it."

Larry didn't waste any time showing Bud other technologies all around the lab, and Bud's head soon spun with information overload as Larry told him about the equipment spread throughout the laboratory.

"So how am I ever going to learn how all this stuff works?" asked Bud, feeling completely overwhelmed.

"Well, B-man ... you don't mind if I call you B-man, do you?" Larry asked.

Bud shook his head no.

"Here is lesson *numero uno* for you: just try to figure it out on your own. When you get completely stuck, ask me, but not one minute sooner, and definitely don't ask me unless you've tried at least three possible solutions using what you've already learned. Because I might just ask you to show me what you tried already. Got it?"

"But—" started Bud.

Larry interrupted, "No ifs, ands, or buts. All our butts need to be seated at a workbench working on solving the 'ifs' and 'ors.' Got it?"

Bud gave Larry a half smile. "Got it," Bud said as he took a deep breath and sat down at the workbench.

"Now let me tell you about my own special three golden rules," Larry said.

— 4 —

Bud's trips to the Space Center turned into a regular weekend routine. Bud was happy to have time with his father, even if it was only during the ride to the Space Center, but what really excited him was being called the youngest intern in Space Center history. He loved working with Larry in his technoforest, learning about electronics, computers, and the mechanical devices Larry had around his lab. Larry was a much better teacher then boring Ms. Ferguson, and besides, Bud really enjoyed learning how things worked and was getting better and better at it.

Along with learning new things, Bud was also gaining confidence with each trip to the Space Center as he built new contraptions. He appreciated Larry's teaching approach, which helped him learn that he could solve any problem that came his way by staying focused and applying Larry's three golden rules, even when solving problems involved learning boring Ms. Ferguson's prepositions and verbs during regular school days.

Bud reflected on Larry's three golden rules: observe carefully; determine the problem to be solved; and solve the problem using trial and error. Larry had another rule, which was to avoid jumping to a quick solution by listening too much to the opinions of others, but Bud's father already had taught him that one.

During one of his weekend trips to the Space Center, Bud tinkered with an electronic circuit board next to Larry on a workbench.

"I was thinking," Bud said. "I have this cool tree house, and I'm trying to get power to it for my computer, lights, and other things I want to do in it. I thought about using my dad's extension cord, but it's not long enough. I'm a bit stuck. Any ideas?"

Larry thought about it for a minute. "Have you applied the three golden rules already?" Larry asked.

Bud nodded. "But I need more information before I can apply the third rule."

"Which is what?" Larry prompted.

"Use trial and error to solve the problem," Bud recited.

Larry smiled. "Very good." He looked around the lab. "You need to use batteries … big batteries." Larry went on to explain basic chemistry of batteries to Bud and how to build a basic battery from raw materials.

Bud started experimenting with what Larry taught him. He grabbed a handful of supplies from a drawer, including pennies, chucks of aluminum foil, paper towels, a cardboard roll, and a plastic spray bottle labeled "lemon juice." He combined the pennies, chunks of aluminum foil, and some paper towels sprayed with lemon juice, then rolled the stack up into the cardboard tube. He touched one side of the crude battery to a small light.

"This is the positive side, and this one is the negative side," Bud said as he attached the negative side of the crude battery to a small light using a couple of thin wires. The light glowed when Bud attached the wires.

He grinned. "Power from pennies and lemon juice. Nice."

It wasn't long before Bud was making batteries from empty plastic milk containers filled with saltwater to see how much electricity he could generate. Bud had spread the plastic bottles around Larry's lab, and each had a piece of copper and a galvanized nail in it, along with a mixture of salt and water.

Bud checked the voltage with a meter, which displayed in large numbers how much electricity he had generated and how many lights he could get to glow, but Bud became frustrated. No matter how hard he tried, he still could not store enough electricity to power up a computer, let alone the other electronic devices he wanted to use in his tree house.

Bud found Larry in the back of the lab, where he was working on his bubbling-brew contraption.

"I still can't generate enough electricity for the equipment I want to power up in my tree house," Bud told him in irritation.

Larry looked at Bud with a mischievous expression and a half smile. "Well," Larry said as he rubbed his chin, "I think you're ready for something new now. Do you know what made the batteries work when you placed a piece of copper and a galvanized nail in each bottle of saltwater?"

"Sure thing. Electricity is caused by the chemical reaction. When I connect the light, the circuit is completed, and the light glows."

"Very good," Larry said with a sparkle in his eyes.

Bud gave Larry an impatient look and said, "Sure, it's great that I know all that, but as James T. Kirk said, I need more power, man!"

Larry laughed. "Okay, right. Well, there's another technology that can generate much more power, and you can run it off water … but I wasn't sure you were ready for it."

"It will run off water? Really? Water?" repeated Bud.

"Yes, B-man—water. It is called a hydrogen-powered fuel cell … the kind they use to operate the latest electric cars—and, well, my space vehicles."

Bud remembered the large glass container in the back of the laboratory with the word "hydrogen" on it. "You mean, you put gasoline into a cell or something?" asked Bud impatiently. "What's the point? Why not just use gasoline?"

"Well, no, not exactly. Let me explain. You generate the hydrogen from water and then use the hydrogen as the fuel. So let me back up. I've been experimenting with various materials, and I think I have come up with a fuel cell that would also work nicely in your tree house. It uses hydrogen, or what they call a green technology fuel."

Bud, still confused, gave Larry a blank stare.

"Stay with me now, B-man. Focus. My latest fuel-cell design generates much more power than previous fuel-cell designs," continued Larry in his fast-talking engineer voice, his eyes widening like those of a crazy scientist.

"That all sounds cool, but why is it green fuel? That sounds gross."

"It's green because it is good for the environment." Larry pulled out a small science kit. "Bought this for you," he told Bud. "Just didn't think you'd be ready for it so quick." The front of the box showed a plastic car.

"It's a toy car that uses a fuel cell to generate electricity from hydrogen. In other words, it uses hydrogen instead of fossil fuels like gasoline. That makes it good for the environment," Larry explained as he placed the science kit on the workbench. "Here are the instructions. I'm sure you can figure it out," he said as the phone on his belt started to vibrate wildly. "Darn—need to run to a meeting. Consider it your next project." Larry dashed out of the room.

Bud placed the parts in the box on his workbench and started reading the instructions aloud. "A small plastic stand allows the wheels to turn when a small motor receives electricity from the fuel cell. A square fuel cell is mounted into the car." He began assembling the kit.

The car had a clear plastic box mounted on the back of it with two plastic circular chambers, one large and one small. "First, we put some ordinary tap water in the plastic fuel containers." Bud poured some of the ice water he had been drinking into both containers.

"Next, we apply power from a small battery to the fuel cell. The battery applies an electric current to the water. This is called e-lec-trol-y-sis," Bud said slowly as he pronounced the strange new word. He connected the battery according to the diagram in the directions. "Next, the electricity from the battery causes a chemical reaction in the water, splitting the H_2O molecule into two atoms of hydrogen and one atom of oxygen. So that means the bubbles in the large container are bubbles of hydrogen?" Bud looked at the large container closely. The water in both containers was bubbling slowly. "Huh. Both containers look the same to me. I need something that can prove there's hydrogen in the large container."

Bud looked around the workbench and then opened up a drawer and moved around the contents. He found a metal device with "Spark" stamped in it. He grabbed the handle and squeezed; a spark came out of the top. "Cool—this thing generates a spark. Must be used for welding or something. I wonder …"

Bud took a plastic tube off the large container; the water inside it was still bubbling. He moved his face close to the large container to get a good look as he put the metal device near where the plastic tube had been connected. He squeezed the metal device, generating a spark.

Whoosh! The hydrogen ignited in a small, blue flash. Bud jumped back and grabbed his face. Luckily, he hadn't gotten burned, but his eyebrows and eyelashes were now curled-up stubs.

"Wow! That was totally cool." Suddenly, a lightbulb turned on in Bud's head. "Aha!" Bud said. "Electrolysis generates bubbles of hydrogen and bubbles of oxygen. Then the fuel cell converts the bubbles of hydrogen to generate electricity. Who knew?"

Bud looked closely at the plastic car as water continued to bubble into the large plastic chamber. He continued reading the instructions. "Collect the hydrogen and then disconnect the battery to stop the electrolysis. Next, connect the toy car motor to the fuel cell's positive and negative terminals."

Bud followed the directions and then jumped as the motor started turning suddenly, causing the car wheels to rotate quickly, shooting the car forward like a bullet. It launched itself off the workbench and fell hard onto the floor, landing on its wheels and shooting across the room until it finally ran head-on into the solid brick wall of the laboratory with a thud. Incredibly, the little vehicle stayed in one piece.

Bud's eyes grew as big as saucers. "Holy cow! So that little car is running on hydrogen. I just generated hydrogen fuel from water—way cool!" Bud picked up the car, with its wheels still spinning fast, and placed it on the floor facing the other direction.

Larry had just walked into the room and was staring at the screen of his phone when the small plastic car zoomed toward him. He jumped when the car smacked into his foot, almost dropping his overused cell phone.

"I see you figured it out while I was in my meeting," Larry said, grinning. "That was pretty quick, B-man. You trying to get a promotion—" Larry stopped midsentence as he noticed Bud's stubby eyebrows. He cleared his throat. "I see you discovered hydrogen is flammable, too."

Bud just looked at Larry with a blank stare. He then said impatiently, "Now will you show me how to power up my entire tree house?"

Larry grinned at Bud and shook his head. "You have got to be the most focused and determined kid I have ever met." Larry pulled out another large box full of parts from under a nearby workbench. "These components should do it," Larry said. "I designed these fuel cells as prototypes for a space-probe project a year ago that got canceled. Each one of these small fuel cells generates the same amount of power as a car battery. You put enough of these puppies together along with this little old inverter device, and we will have your tree house lit up brighter than a Christmas tree!"

Larry gathered some of the equipment Bud would need and set it aside on the workbench. "I need to get a few more components for you, but it'll have to wait 'til later." Larry looked down at his phone again. "I'll drop it all off later tonight when I get off work. Look for it next to your tree house, along with some instructions on how to put it together. I'm sure you'll be able to figure it out," Larry said absently without looking up, shaking his head at his phone.

"Sure thing, just like always," Bud said as he rolled his eyes and smiled, imagining how his tree house might look all lit up.

"I've created a monster," Larry said, giving Bud a quick glance. "Oh, shoot—I'm late for my next meeting."

Bud just grinned and looked at the plastic car he held in his hands as the wheels continued to spin.

— 5 —

THE WHEEL ON THE old bicycle was spinning fast now on top of Bud's sprawling tree house, two stories from the ground. Bud tightened the rope he was using as a pulley to turn the generator Larry had given him. It was getting dark now.

"There … and there … a little more … perfect," Bud said making the final adjustments to his tree house. The generator started to make a low-pitched humming sound as Bud looked with anticipation at the main power switch. He followed the wires firmly secured to the old oak tree upward with his eyes one last time, making sure everything was ready. Bud looked again at the power switch secured to the thick trunk of the oak tree. The long, wooden paddles he had attached on top of the oak tree started to rotate as the wind pushed them. The paddles connected to the other end of the rope he had just tightened now rotated faster, cutting through the air, whistling loudly as the wind pushed them harder. The sun had just gone down, and the wind was blowing unusually hard on this warm fall evening.

Bud looked around his tree house. Wires connected to the lightbulbs had been meticulously placed all around the three-room tree house. On the newly installed computer, Bud could play video games or watch the army of deployed wireless webcams he had placed all around his yard. An old ham radio Larry had given him sat in another corner of the tree house.

Bud looked below with pride at the small power generator connected to a maze of plastic piping he had designed. Pipes of hydrogen went to the fuel cells. Wind power turned the paddles, which also turned the generator, keeping the electrolysis going and generating more hydrogen. Below his tree house, Bud had lined up a bunch of old five-gallon containers Larry had given him to store the hydrogen he had generated. The containers were linked with plastic PVC pipes circling around the containers to the fuel cells that generated electricity. Bud had connected thick wires to the fuel cells that he ran up the side of the oak-tree trunk to a circuit breaker, distributing power to each plywood room of the tree house.

Bud looked around his tree house. Its wires and pipes and newly installed light fixtures amounted to an impressive sight; one of his inventor heroes, Nikola Tesla, would have been impressed, he thought.

"Well, here goes nothin'," Bud mumbled, taking a deep breath. He flipped the switch to "On."

With a flash, the tree house transformed from a dark, wooden structure integrated into the large oak tree into a brightly lit wooden lighthouse seemingly floating two stories above the ground.

"Yeah! Way cool! It worked!" yelled Bud. He took out his cell phone and tapped a few things on the screen.

The lights went off. He tapped again; the lights went back on. He tapped again, and the computer came on. He tapped again, and the ham radio came on. A few more taps caused the old ham radio to tune to a predefined frequency that Larry monitored.

"Larry, can you hear me?" Bud said at the top of his lungs as he looked upward toward the microphone positioned above his head. "Larry, over. Can you hear me? Over."

"You don't have to yell, B-man. I read, over," responded Larry.

"It worked … it really worked! Over!" Bud still could not believe it. After all the hard work he had put into this old tree house project, it was finally working.

"I am now receiving a video stream over the Internet from your webcams, Bud," Larry reported in a monotone Mission Control fashion. "All systems are operational. All systems are go. Over."

"Bu-ud! Bu-ud! Hey Bu-ud! Dinnertime!" shouted Sara from the back door of their house, far below the tree house. Bud could smell the unmistakable scent of the home-cooked meatloaf Grams had made for dinner. His stomach growled.

"Very impressive—nice work!" Larry said. "Congratulations, now you have your own technotree of sorts."

Larry was the best teacher Bud ever had known. Bud smiled with his hands on his hips as he looked around again. "Thanks for all your help. Gotta go. Bud out."

— 6 —

Bud followed his father into his office at the Space Center. Bud kept an eye on his cell phone display as he navigated toward the small table and chair adjacent to his father's desk.

His father sat down in the large, padded leather desk chair and started typing on his computer. Bud was spending more time at his father's office now that he was helping Larry with real projects as an official Space Center intern. Bud was pretty proud of being called a Space Center Intern.

His father's assistant ran into the office, out of breath. "Dr. Thompson. We need to show you our latest readings." The assistant motioned for him to come quickly.

Bud watched his father promptly follow the assistant into the computer lab. He didn't ask if he could follow. He just did, while struggling to keep up. It wasn't long before he was stretching his neck, looking over his father's shoulder at the computer screen.

The scientists looked at the information again as Bud's father sat in front of the computer displaying the graphical map data they were all so interested in. Bud's father tapped on the computer screen and looked more closely at the data as Bud tried to see what his father was looking at.

"Amazing! I can't believe it," said Bud's father. "It's a lake over 175 miles long and 40 miles across. Its volume is nearly 4,000 cubic miles. It looks to be far larger than the size of Lake Superior. And look here … the depth would be similar to—oh, my—Lake Tahoe."

"Where is that?" Bud asked.

"This is an image of a temperature map from our new satellite. It's showing a warm-water lake under the ice in West Antarctica," Bud's father said.

"A lake in Antarctica? Isn't everything frozen there?" asked Bud.

"Well, yes. But lakes aren't that unusual under miles of ice in Antarctica. There are probably over seventy of them. But this lake is very different; this one is showing a temperature of 70 degrees Fahrenheit." His father pressed a few keys, and the image changed to a three-dimensional image of the Antarctic lake they had just discovered. He leaned in, squinting at the computer screen, his eyes locked on what he was seeing. "These three-dimensional images show an unusually large temperature anomaly here in the middle of the Western Antarctic. You can see the sizable mass with its western edge inland from Sobral," Bud's father said, talking to the other scientists.

"Sobral?" interrupted Bud.

"Oh, ah, Sobral is one of the Argentinean National Antarctic Data Centers," replied his father as he continued to stare at the computer screen.

His father looked at his assistant. "The data shows that this lake is larger than Lake Vostok and much, much warmer!"

"Vostok?" asked Bud, interrupting again.

His father sighed and whispered, "Yes, Bud, Lake Vostok. It's another large lake under the ice in Antarctica. But Vostok is a very cold lake—"

"A large warm-water lake under two miles of ice in the middle of Antarctica?" interrupted his assistant. "C'mon, Dr. Thompson, this data has got to be wrong. Why didn't it show up in earlier mapping missions?"

"Well, obviously, Google's Advanced Inner Earth Discovery Satellite provides much more detail and image resolution than ever before," Bud's father replied. "It appears that there are some very large temperature anomalies under the ice sheet in this specific region. Look here. Now, look at this satellite image. Here and here." Bud's father pointed to the image correlating the satellite telemetry data with the three-dimensional heat map image on his large computer screen. He then selected the image with the mouse, and a three-dimensional image of the warm-water lake appeared.

"You're right; it is another large lake. But this one is different," said his assistant. "Look, this data shows a layer deeper than where the existing lakes had been mapped, and it has a temperature anomaly. It is indicating a huge space—most likely another lake—with a temperature at around 70 degrees Fahrenheit, or 21 degrees Celsius." His father's assistant paused, looking perplexed.

"But why isn't that water near the freezing point, like all the other lakes below the ice we've mapped to date?" his assistant asked bluntly. "The average temperature reading of Lake Vostok is about 27 degrees Fahrenheit, or –3 Celsius. These temperature readings are very strange."

Bud looked at the computer screen and then at his father, who appeared completely shocked by the data.

Bud knew by the look on his father's face that something was wrong.

"If they're correct … can that lake sustain any form of life?" asked his assistant.

Finally, his father took a deep breath and then smiled and said, "You have got to be kidding. After millions of years, I'm sure all we'll find in that lake are clumps of prehistoric sediment. But I do agree that these temperature anomalies are very puzzling."

Another scientist walked in, holding a large paper printout. "The temperature readings are confirmed. We have a very large, warm-water lake anomaly deep under the Western Antarctic ice sheet, extending deep into the earth."

Bud moved his face closer to the computer screen as if it might help him understand the 3-D images he was seeing of the warm-water lake far below the ice in Antarctica.

"We need to report this immediately," said his father to the scientists. "We must be able to explain this information to the Jet Propulsion Laboratory—or JPL, as you probably usually hear me refer to it—and NASA." He paused and then looked at Bud. "Will you call your grandmother? Tell her we'll be late tonight."

"Sure thing, Dad," Bud said, feeling cooler by the minute.

7

Bud and Gregory sat comfortably in the old leather chairs in the tree house, watching the small television Gregory had contributed to their home away from home. They were now hanging out at the tree house every day after school.

Bud was proud of his green-powered tree house and got satisfaction out of the fact that Gregory had no idea how he was able to power up his entire tree house using only water. Bud knew it wasn't just water that powered the tree house, but he liked how he felt when Gregory watched him stick the garden hose into the metal tank he used for electrolysis.

Bud picked up his fancy cell phone. "Hey, check this out." Bud tapped a few buttons, and a buzzing sound came from above them.

Gregory twisted his head to look above them. "What the heck?"

Bud smiled and tapped several more times on his cell phone. A flying remote-controlled helicopter buzzed closely over the top of Gregory's head, surprising him.

"Hey, watch it!" Gregory said as he swatted at the fast-moving helicopter. "When did you get the RC heli?"

"It's not what it seems. Check this out." Bud tapped his cell phone, and the helicopter flew above them and hovered in one spot. Bud handed the cell phone to Gregory.

The screen showed a live video image that was coming from the helicopter and playing on the cell phone's screen. "Cool—that's us! So that thing takes pictures?"

Bud nodded. "And much more. It takes video and sound and transmits it to my cell phone. Cool, huh?"

Gregory looked at the image and then handed the phone back to Bud. "You have got to be the coolest geek in school. This is one of your best inventions yet."

Bud was proud of and excited about his recent inventions; Larry had taught him well. Unable to help himself, he bragged a little. "I have one in my dad's office, too. I'm going to surprise him with it. Let me activate it and try to get his attention." Bud tapped on the cell phone a few times, and an image appeared from the helicopter Bud had positioned on the top shelf of the cluttered bookshelf against the wall directly behind his father's desk chair.

The helicopter sat firmly in place, transmitting video and audio in real time. An image appeared on Bud's cell phone. It showed the back of his father's head and the computer screen on his desk. Suddenly a message appeared on his father's screen, along with a loud beep: "Incoming conference call."

Bud thought for a moment about disconnecting the cell phone, since he had never intended to spy on his father. He hesitated, considering disconnecting the line, but his curiosity kept him watching.

Gregory squeezed in so he could see the cell-phone screen, too.

"Looks like a conference call is going to start. I wonder who's calling," Bud said.

"Are you crazy, dude? Your dad is gonna kill you if he finds out you were spying on him."

"Ah, only for a minute or two—I'm sure he won't mind. After all, I'm not spying on him ... just testing a prototype, as Larry would say. After all, I am an intern—"

Suddenly, his father turned around. Bud jumped; he thought for sure his father was looking into the camera on the helicopter, but Bud's father just got up to shut his office door instead before returning to his desk.

Bud took a deep breath.

The two boys could see only the back of Bud's father's head, but they had a clear view of the computer screen. Bud tapped the cell screen and zoomed in until the computer screen filled the cell phone's display. Again, Bud tapped his cell phone, setting up the directional microphone on the helicopter so Bud and Gregory could hear what was being said in his father's office.

An image of a conference room appeared with a large Seal of the President displayed on the wall. The room was dimly lit, with running lights around the perimeter and a large screen at the front of the room displaying a bright map of Antarctica. Air conditioning blew out of the ceiling vents, causing the little streamers attached to the vents to dance wildly.

"Good morning, Dr. Thompson. I am glad you can join us on your secure line," said Colonel Jerry Williams, an African American military man. He wore a United States Air Force uniform, displaying the full-bird colonel insignias on his shoulders and above the mass of colorful ribbons on his chest, which signified more than thirty years of military service. Even though Bud was looking at the small display screen on his cell phone, the lines on Colonel William's clean-shaven, rough face and graying hair reinforced his military years of experience.

"Some secure line," Gregory said as he chuckled.

Bud looked at Gregory with a serious expression, and his finger hovered over the "Disconnect" button.

"Dude, don't. This is way cool," Gregory said.

Bud thought about it again for a moment. "Okay. I have an idea," Bud said, quickly walking over to the beat-up desk and pressing a couple of keys on the computer keyboard. With a beep, the video on his cell phone magically appeared on the screen of the small television sitting next to the computer.

"No way ... how'd you do that?"

Bud grinned as both boys got closer to the television screen.

Colonel Williams rubbed his hands together. "Ironic," he said as he pointed at the map of Antarctica.

"Excuse me, Colonel?" Bud's father said.

"Oh, sorry, Dr. Thompson. Just talking to myself. It feels like Antarctica in this room today," replied Colonel Williams as he looked into the camera. Colonel William's face filled Bud's father's computer screen and Bud's television screen at the same time.

"You're alone, Dr. Thompson ... correct?" asked Colonel Williams.

Bud and Gregory looked at each other again with raised eyebrows. Bud looked at the cell phone again and was seriously considering tapping the "Disconnect" button when Gregory pleaded, "Dude, please—this is really cool. I am totally into this now. Let's keep watching!"

Bud thought for a moment and then put the cell phone down.

"Yes, Colonel. Of course," Bud's father said.

A group of twelve highly decorated military men and women, along with four civilian men dressed in recently pressed black suits, burst into the room as if they were late for the meeting, taking their seats around the large conference table and flipping through the documentation placed in front of them.

"Dang!" Gregory said. "Look the front covers of their binders. They all have "Top Secret" printed on them."

"Oh man, am I in trouble! Let's—"

Gregory interrupted. "C'mon, dude, don't disconnect. It's really getting good now."

Bud couldn't help himself; they both kept watching.

A door suddenly opened in the back of the room.

"Attention!" barked the impeccably dressed military policeman standing next to the door. The president of the United States walked in, with another man dressed in a wrinkled gray suit following closely behind.

"Holy Donkey Kong," Bud said as both boys remained completely fixated on the television screen.

Colonel Williams stood at attention and saluted.

"At ease," said the president of the United States. "Colonel, please proceed. I have a press conference in fifteen minutes."

"Thank you, Mr. President," said Colonel Williams in a deep baritone voice. The colonel addressed the room: "Please turn to the first page of the briefing in front of you."

The rustling of papers echoed in the room as each person around the table turned the pages of their briefing document.

"As most of you know," the colonel continued, "a consortium of nine UK universities, plus the British Antarctica Survey and the National Oceanography Centre, received funding in 2009 to develop technology that could drill through the West Antarctica ice sheet down to Lake Ellisworth, nearly 3 kilometers, or 1.8 miles, under the ice, without disrupting the pristine environment. Around the same time, the University of Washington in Seattle used NASA's ICESat's laser technology to provide a complete map of Antarctica's ice sheets, revealing an extensive network of channels, some over hundreds of kilometers long. That same year, JPL teamed up with Google in order to develop the Advanced Inner Earth Discovery Satellite—"

The president looked over at the NASA director, who appeared surprised. The president interrupted the colonel to address the NASA director: "This was by my direction, Frank. Having Google assist in the effort helped me explain why we were spending so much doggone money on 'ice' research."

"That's the president talking. This is unbelievable," remarked Gregory.

Bud just sat there, watching nervously, and realized he was holding his breath. He let it out.

Colonel Williams continued, "Yes, sir. The satellite is designed to penetrate the earth more deeply and with more detail than all the previous technologies."

Bud was starting to feel even more nervous now. His hands started to tremble. "I need to disconnect this thing," Bud said as he picked up the phone.

"Ah, man, please? Just for one more minute, okay?"

Bud let out another long breath and nodded.

"Google's first deployment of the data collected from the bird over Antarctica provided penetrating maps of the earth. As you all know, Google called it the virtual Google Center to the Earth Journey, and this name quickly went viral. Just last year, NASA began using the technology to map the inner layers of the moon and Mars. In partnership with academia, we gave a scientist named Dr. John Thompson satellite time to point the bird toward Antarctica. I should also point out that Dr. Thompson is with us here today. His team is the one who made this remarkable warm-water lake discovery."

Bud could tell the president was looking closely at the video box of his father on the screen. Bud smiled.

Colonel Williams continued, "We cleared Dr. John Thompson as the lead scientist for the Antarctic expedition. He has been working with the NASA and JPL teams to define the equipment and procedures that will be used for the drilling expedition—"

The president interrupted again. "Williams, would ya stop chewin' the fat? What's the present status of this project? Give it to us in plain English, would you?" demanded the president in a southern accent as he moved restlessly in his firmly padded boardroom chair, looking at his watch. "Time's ticking, Colonel."

Colonel Williams went on. "Yes, sir, Mr. President. Certainly. Finland, Norway, and Uruguay tried to derail the project, throwing their nontechnical two cents into the mix regarding environmental concerns. The Saudis also announced their desire that the new lake be left untouched forever for religious reasons. But Dr. Thompson was able to get the international community's approval of the environmentally friendly tools and technology that will be used to drill into the Antarctic ice, along with a high-tech probe to sample the waters of the lake."

Just then, the helicopter on the shelf in Bud's father's office jerked and made a noise as a gear moved slightly. Bud's father turned around in front of the screen as he looked in the direction of the helicopter.

"No way! The helicopter moved!" Gregory shouted. Bud looked at the television screen in panic. He grabbed his cell phone and tapped on it a few times, shifting to a widescreen view of the entire room. His father turned back around toward his computer screen.

Bud took a deep breath and zoomed back in to his father's computer screen.

The president interrupted Colonel Williams again. "Let me be clear, ladies and gentlemen: before we count our chickens, international relations are *as* important as that little ol' frozen lake under that frozen slab of ice down yonder. No disrespect, Dr. Thompson. Now, as you were saying, Williams? Get on with it."

"Yes, sir. I am assigned to oversight duty for the American team—" started Colonel Williams.

The president interrupted again. "My orders to Colonel Williams are clear. This is like two goats in a pepper patch with the international community, so the colonel needs to stay out of the way of the other teams, and that goes for the rest of y'all. Got it?" said the president as he looked around the room.

Colonel Williams nodded and continued. "The Russians have joined the expedition, and the combined New Zealand and Australian teams signed up shortly after the Russians to form the combined United States,

Russian, and Australian Antarctic Lake Expedition Team—or URA, as we call them. The only loose end is Argentina. They're making demands and claims regarding territory and the expedition site's location. We continue to ignore them, since we don't recognize their territory. They sat out of the talks in protest, which also caused them to miss out on the earmarks distributed to the rest of the members. You might say they're extremely agitated at the moment. Rumors are that they want to take back what they think is their territory."

The president spoke up again, this time sitting up straight in his chair and appearing very focused. He looked over to the older man in a black pressed suit with "CIA Director" printed on the name placard in front of him.

"Jones, do we have someone in—"

"Yes, sir," the CIA director interrupted. "In the Argentinean general's office, Mr. President."

"Did you see his name tag?" Gregory exclaimed. "The CIA? Really? OMG! The CIA?"

Bud shook his head nervously and forced another breath.

Colonel Williams continued, "Cal Tech, NASA, and JPL established a probe-development team. The probe will be lowered down through a borehole made by the drill and will take data samples and transmit it back to the surface of the ice, two miles above. A small Internet-enabled digital camera and lighting system will be mounted inside the probe. Filtered, nonsecure data will be broadcast over the Internet, where research teams around the world can analyze the data after a short delay. We have flown in equipment, tools, supplies, and personnel into the middle of Antarctica. The expedition camp at the drill site is now ready. Dr. Thompson, are you ready to leave for the site, so we can commence drilling?"

Bud's eyes grew as big as saucers. "Really?" Bud said loudly to the television set, as if they could hear him. Again he said, "Really?"

"Yes, Colonel, I'm ready," Bud's father said.

"Good. Mr. President, Dr. Thompson will also be bringing his children on-site, along with many of the other team members—all approved by the URA. In fact, the URA even approved the request for Dr. Thompson to bring his family dog," said Colonel Williams, and then in the same breath he added, "We're go, Mr. President."

The president nodded. "Well, butter my biscuit, Colonel. It sounds like we're goin' to the dance! Proceed, Williams." The president stood up.

"Dude, you're going to Antarctica," Gregory told Bud. "Way cool! Did you know that?"

Bud shook his head nervously. Completely shocked, he continued watching without saying a word.

"Thank you, Colonel Williams. Keep me up to date, and whatever you do, stay the heck out of the pepper patch. I don't want to hear about any ruffled feathers down there. Let those civilians explore. You got it?" said the president in a serious tone, though his southern accent softened the impact. The president looked into the camera and gave Bud's father a big wink.

Bud disconnected the link. Bud and Gregory sat down and looked at each other.

"What the heck did the president mean? He lost me with pepper patch and ruffled feathers," said Gregory.

Bud took a deep breath. "Guess he wants the military guys to stay away, so my father's scientists can do research." Bud stood up, still in shock from what he had just heard. "Looks like I'm goin' on a trip."

— 8 —

Bud hit his alarm and sent it on a flight off the nightstand. "5:00 a.m. already?" The wintry chill in the room encouraged Bud to stay a little longer under the warm covers as his head slowly fell back onto the pillow. Bud mumbled with his eyes still closed, "Summer ... it's summer now in Antarctica."

Bud's eyes popped open. "This is going to be wicked cool!" Bud was already dressed when he jumped out of bed. He grabbed his already packed, overstuffed duffel bag and headed toward the stairs, dragging it behind him. He passed Sara's room and noticed her sitting on the corner of her bed with a faraway look in her teary eyes. He moved faster to avoid her, since he knew that talking to her would mean he'd have to hear her loud complaints all over again: "I'll be missing the last six months of high school! And my prom! I can't leave my friends—I just can't!"

"Bud!" yelled his father. "Please get Casey and his kennel. I have his food already."

Bud dragged his duffel bag down the stairs one thump at a time. He placed it next to the other bags his father had stacked by the door. "Okay. No need to yell. I'm right here," Bud said as he stood behind his father with the dog kennel in his hand and Casey following him. "This is going to be cool, Case!" Bud told the dog. "We're goin' on a trip! C'mere, Case."

Casey gave Bud a double take and then started a game of keep-away, hobbling around the room and flinging slobber everywhere as Bud tried to corral him. Luckily for Casey, Bud's father had convincingly argued that Casey was getting on in years and should be allowed to go on the expedition with them. He had received the green light to bring the dog; after all, his father was the mission commander and in charge of the expedition.

Grams moved frantically around the house, picking up one thing and helping them pack another.

"Gonna miss your home cooking, Grams. Why aren't you coming with us?" asked Bud as he finally grabbed Casey.

"I'm going to miss you too, child, but I need to take care of things here for your father while you're away. Besides, a trip with your father will be very exciting for you children."

"Yeah, right," Sara said as she threw her bag on top of Bud's.

Bud knew he needed to stay as far away from his sister as possible for the moment, so he did his best to back away.

"Children, please put your jackets on before you go outside," said Grams softly. She was starting to tear up. "I'm going to miss everyone terribly."

Casey got away from Bud, grabbed one of Bud's shoes, and took off toward the stairs. Bud was getting more frustrated by the minute. Casey went most places with Bud, lagging behind him as Bud cruised on his bike with Gregory (bumping into anything in his path) and hanging out with him in the tree house. Still, Casey had a mind of his own most of the time.

"Casey! Sit! Stay! Bud said in the deepest voice he could muster as he made an arm motion for Casey to sit. Casey froze, dropped the shoe, and then sat.

"What about your tree house?" asked Grams. "Do I need to tend to it?"

"No. Gregory volunteered. He'll be hanging out in it after school," Bud grunted as he put on his shoe.

Grams nodded and handed Bud his baseball cap.

After a few frantic minutes, they were all finally loaded up and in the taxi, going to the Executive Air Terminal to board the special chartered plane to Antarctica. Bud took a deep breath as the taxi pulled away.

We're finally on our adventure to Antarctica, he thought.

"Just like old times," Bud said out loud.

Everyone, even Casey, got quiet as Bud quickly realized he shouldn't have made that comment. His comment prompted Sara to get tears in her eyes. "I wish Mom were with us," she said, her bottom lip quivering.

Bud just ignored her and looked out of the back window of the beat-up yellow taxi at their house growing smaller as they slowly drove away. He missed his mother, too. He tried not to think about that very often, although he carried a picture of the two of them, taken years ago, in his right front pocket everywhere he went. He pulled out the worn and tattered picture, looked at it for a few moments, took a deep breath, and then tucked it away back in his pocket.

Suddenly Casey surprised him with a big lick on his cheek. "Ugh, Case, that's gross," Bud said, but he couldn't help but smile.

Then Casey sneezed violently twice, surprising everyone again as big gobs of disgusting slobber flew everywhere. Even the cab driver looked back in disgust.

Bud looked at his father and then at Sara as they all wiped the slobber off themselves. Both Sara and his father were looking at him and making faces as Bud tried to wipe up the mess all around them, but it was just too funny. Bud started laughing, Sara started laughing, and even their father joined in. Everyone was laughing hard—except for the taxi driver. Bud assumed that was either because the taxi driver realized he had some gross cleanup to do inside his taxicab or because he just had no idea what they were saying.

Finally, Bud thought, *now this is like old times.*

— 9 —

THE FLIGHT TO THE camp had seemed to take days. The cold Antarctic wind was blowing hard when the plane arrived on final approach, bouncing the plane around violently.

Bud felt as if he were on a roller coaster and turned at least three different shades of green as his motion sickness intensified. He tried hard to focus his eyes on a single spot, then closed them and tried to hold still as the plane seemed to roll, pitch, and yaw all at once, causing his head to spin like a badly thrown Frisbee.

Relief finally came as the plane touched down hard, bouncing three times on the long, solid runway carved out of the thick ice sheet adjacent to the expedition camp.

The pilot made an announcement over the intercom. "Welcome to URA Expedition Camp. It is shortly after midnight."

"Oh, boy, we're here," Sara said sarcastically when they finally came to a stop. She had been cranky for the entire trip.

"Doesn't look like midnight—looks like late afternoon, if you ask me," Bud said as he looked at the sunlight

50

gently touching the tents and landscape surrounding the expedition camp out of his tiny airplane window.

"No one asked you," thundered back Sara.

Bud just ignored her. "Man, there must be a hundred people out there," Bud said.

Bud's father leaned over to get a good view. "See over there—those large shelled structures that are elevated above the ice? Those are what they call hard-shell expedition tents," Bud's father said, pointing past the people frantically moving around below them.

"They don't look like the camping tents I remember," Bud said, grinning. "From the looks of what those people are wearing and those flags blowing around, the arctic wind must be pretty cold," he added.

As if on cue, the pilot made another announcement: "Just in case you're wondering, the outside temperature is −60 degrees Fahrenheit, which is −51 degrees Celsius. But not to worry, you will be using the jet bridge leading directly inside the facility to a comfortable 68 degrees Fahrenheit … just like home."

Bud rolled his eyes.

They made their way through the loosely attached jet bridge, which bounced as they walked toward the US team's expedition tent. There, the family was greeted by busy team members, who quickly returned to their work. Casey barked and limped around with foaming drool oozing from his wide-open mouth.

"Hey, Casey—no, no!" yelled Bud. Casey started to walk in a circle and then began moving quickly from left to right. "Casey, no!" yelled Bud again. "Dad, Casey needs to go poop. Where should I take him?"

Dr. Kurt Popov, the Russian camp facilitator, greeted them just in time to see what Casey was planning to do.

He looked at Casey briefly with disgust before turning his attention to Bud's father.

"Dr. Thompson?"

"Yes, that's me. This is my daughter, Sara, and this is my son, Bud and ... well, that's our, ah, dog, Casey." Casey continued to sniff around, searching for a place to relieve himself.

"Good to meet you. My name is Dr. Kurt Popov. I am the camp facilitator and will be your assistant on this exped—"

Bud's father interrupted. "Ah, is there someplace we can take our dog? He obviously has had a long trip."

"*Da*. Just outside the main tent structure, in the temperature-controlled area, is fine for now. Just let a team member know they need to clean up." Kurt pointed to a nearby door and then to one of the maintenance men walking by them.

Kurt was an older Russian gentleman with receding white hair and wire-rimmed glasses. He looked very distinguished as he carefully pronounced each syllable of each word he spoke with a Russian accent, though his English was not perfect. "Comrade, I have heard much about famous Space Center Mission Control director, Dr. John Thompson, while I ran earth sciences department at Lomonosov, Moscow State University, where I used satellite to study Antarctic ice sheet," Kurt said.

Bud looked at his father, who was making a face as he watched Casey relieve himself on the ice just outside the open door of the tent building in the small temperature-controlled area Kurt had pointed out.

"Good to meet you, Kurt," Bud's father said. "Can you show us to our rooms? We're exhausted and, um, well, we all need to use the bathroom." Bud's father glanced at what Casey had left behind.

"Yes. Please follow me," Kurt said quickly and then turned away and proceeded down the hall.

They walked into the large US team tent structure, which was about the size of a football field. The air inside the tent was pleasant. Large heaters circulated hot air throughout the reinforced fiberglass tent structure, which resembled a large office building with its maze of hallways and workrooms.

Bud stopped to look at the expedition layout map on the wall. The American tent structure was arranged in sections: one section for the expedition team members' gear, a section for the camp's supplies, a section for a cafeteria, and one section broken into many small, fully equipped sleeping quarters for the team members. There was a school section and a recreation section with workout equipment as well. Bud shook his head with his hands on his hips, thinking it looked overwhelmingly huge.

"Bud! C'mon. Keep up with us," shouted his father. Sara was already following her father quietly with her head down.

Kurt showed them to their living quarters. There were four rooms: one room for Sara, one room for Bud, and a large room for his father, along with a modest-sized office.

Bud shouted as he explored the rooms, "Dad! Casey has a kennel next to our rooms; it even has a small dog run!" He then returned to the office, where his father and Kurt were still talking. Casey followed Bud, rubbing himself against Kurt's leg as he passed him.

"Again, it's nice to finally meet you and handsome family," Kurt said. "I must get back to my other duties now."

"Nice to meet you, too," Bud's father said with a yawn. "We're going to try and get some shut-eye now."

"The briefing will commence in approximately five hours," Kurt said as he turned toward the door. "My assistant will wake you promptly at 6:00 a.m. I will be working all night shifts trying to ensure proper equipment has been received and set up before drilling begin. If you need me, that is where I will be."

"It's much bigger than I thought," Sara said after Kurt left, in what Bud thought sounded like her first positive-sounding attempt at conversation in a long time.

"I agree with Sara. It sure is bigger than I thought it would be," Bud said as he shot her a smile.

Sara looked away.

"Bud, will you put our gear in our rooms before you go to your room?" asked Bud's father.

"Sure thing." Bud grabbed the luggage and put it in each of their rooms. Five minutes later, everyone was in his or her respective bed, exhausted after their long journey. Casey started to snore as he drooled all over Bud's pillow.

Bud didn't notice; he was snoring, too.

— 10 —

BUD WOKE UP SUDDENLY when he heard a loud knock at the door of their living quarters.

There it was again. Bud sat up to listen.

"Rise and shine, Dr. Thompson. The status meeting is about to start," said one of Kurt's Australian assistants, yelling through the door, "and you're the host, mate."

Bud stretched. He heard his father reply in a loud whisper: "Okay, okay. Thank you."

As Bud's father prepared to leave for the meeting, Bud showed up, dressed and ready to go. "Dad, I want to go, okay?"

Bud's father gave Bud a surprised look and thought about it for a few seconds, which felt like minutes to Bud. "Well, okay, but please stay close to me. I don't even know my way around this place yet, and Casey needs to stay in his kennel."

Bud nodded. "Cool."

"We better write Sara a note," said his father. "Leave it on the table for her."

"Sure thing," Bud said. He quickly scribbled a note to Sara.

Went with Dad. Already fed Case. He just needs to poop.
Bud

The meeting had already started in the large briefing room when Bud's father and Bud entered the room. There were about fifty people in attendance from all of the expedition teams. Kurt was talking to the group when they arrived.

"… that is status of camp and expected timetable for drilling. The probe has been received yesterday, and drilling rigs are now in place and ready. Drilling commences tomorrow at 6:00 a.m. It is expected to last fifteen days before stop for probe insertion," explained Kurt. "Once we're ten feet from ice breakthrough, we insert the probe into rig. The probe follows behind the drill protected by casing." Kurt pointed to the images on the large projection screen and continued, "Outside temperature is −60 degrees Fahrenheit, and rugged tent dome structures are functioning perfectly. This allows work in comfortable 68 degrees Fahrenheit temperature range." Kurt looked over to Bud's father and continued, "I would next introduce Dr. John Thompson, who will be in charge of mission. Dr. Thompson arrived last night with his family."

The team applauded.

Bud worked his way to the back of the room near a large pot of coffee as his father prepared to speak to the crowd. He watched his father at the same time he leaned too close to the coffeepot and accidentally touched it.

"Ouch!" he said, jerking his arm away. A few people looked back, but Bud pretended he hadn't made the noise and focused innocently on his father, who was now at the front of the room.

As his father spoke, Bud quickly became distracted by all there was to see around the room. A large, colorful screen filling an entire wall in the front of the room displayed an animated image of the world. Another screen to its right showed an image of Antarctica with "T minus 15 days" displayed in large red letters. A time clock below it was counting backward. A screen on the left showed a worldwide network with flashing lines going from Antarctica to places around the world. Bud recognized those places. They were the research centers his father had talked about. His attention shifted back to his father at the front of the room.

"... must remember that our number-one priority is to maintain a sterile lake environment while we collect our telemetry data," Bud's father said as he pointed to the large screen in the front of the room, which displayed an image of the world.

Bud noticed ten rows of computer monitors. "Man, this room is big," Bud mumbled. He had never imagined such a huge undertaking in such a large room full of people, all of whom were working on this expedition. The scene reminded him of old pictures his father had showed him of the Apollo missions to the moon and the Mission Control room that guided the Apollo astronauts on space missions.

"... all data collected by the probe will be routed out over the Internet in real time to the scientific community around the world. Major research centers around the world have been assigned to evaluate the data as they receive it ..."

Bud took out his cell phone. "Cool—I have a signal." He sent his friend Gregory a text message.

Arrived at Expedition. In meeting with Dad. Way cool.

Bud tapped "Send" on his cell phone.

As hard as Bud tried to pay attention, he just could not help himself: he was now completely bored with this meeting and was ready to leave. He looked around, plotting his exit.

"… any issues, go to Kurt, and he will bring the major ones to me. That's all I have at the moment. Let's get to our stations and begin the drilling countdown. As Kurt indicated earlier, drilling begins bright and early tomorrow at 6:00 a.m. Now, ladies and gentlemen, let's get to work!"

The audience applauded.

The applause prompted Bud's relief as he realized the briefing was thankfully now over. He grinned at his father; he couldn't wait to explore the expedition camp.

His father headed straight for the coffee machine where Bud was waiting.

"Good job," Bud said as he started to fidget with each knob on the high-tech coffeemaker.

"Thanks, son. It's hard to believe that after so many months of preparing, the drilling is starting." His father shook his head.

"This place is really cool. I'm ready to take a look around," Bud said, gazing around the room at the fancy displays on the walls.

"Just do me a favor," his father said with a serious look on his face.

Bud looked carefully at his father. "Sure, anything."

"Stay out of trouble."

Bud nodded, gave his father a quick hug, and then left abruptly.

— 11 —

BUD STROLLED BACK TO the room to get Casey, passing information posters on the walls of the hallway outlining evacuation procedures and offering a map of the layout of the camp. Since there weren't any windows, it was easy to get disoriented as the white walls of one hallway blended into the next. Then again, there wouldn't have been much to see outside anyway. The large map and arrow that told him, "You Are Here" came in handy as Bud navigated through the similar-looking hallways.

Sara was still sleeping when Bud arrived back at the room.

"I might as well check this place out while I take Casey for a walk," Bud mumbled.

Bud went into the kennel next to their rooms, where Casey was sleeping. "Hey Case, what do ya think of all this?" Bud whispered. "Huh, boy? Wanna go for a walk?"

Casey stood up with his tail wagging back and forth—drooling, as he usually did, all over the floor. He barked, shooting a glob of drool onto Bud's leg.

"Aw, man. Shhhh, Case. Don't want to wake Sara yet and hear her complaining again, now do we? C'mon, let's go." Bud wiped himself off and then attached the leash to Casey's collar. It took a few tries with Casey bouncing up and down with uncontrollable excitement, sending more globs of drool flying here and there.

Bud led Casey down the long, plain hallway that ran perpendicular to their living quarters. Casey pulled hard on the leash at first, but slowed down as he quickly became out of breath. The harder Casey panted, the farther his slobber flew and the more slowly he moved. Bud ended up pulling Casey as the dog fell behind. He quickly decided that pulling Casey was not going to work and disconnected the leash. Casey would now need to keep up on his own; even if he didn't, it would be pretty hard for Casey to get outside the expedition camp anyway.

Off in the distance, Bud thought he heard someone talking. The hallway was made of heavy fiberglass material, but he could still hear the echo of a conversation somewhere ahead of him. As Bud walked down the hall, he felt a slight chill and looked at a temperature display on the wall showing both the inside and outside temperatures. "It's in the upper 60s in here, Case, but outside, it's nearly 60 below zero. Brrrr—man, that's cold."

There it was again: Bud heard more talking. He continued down the hall. The talking became louder as he continued walking. Bud saw an open door and peeked around the corner. There he saw a boy about his age in a wheelchair, typing at a computer terminal. The boy appeared to be talking to his wheelchair.

Bud entered the room slowly, his eyes jumping from one piece of computer equipment to the next. The boy sat with his back toward the door, talking to a face on his computer display.

"… okay, Tom. Thanks. Talk with you later." The computer beeped as the video connection disconnected.

"Hey, whatcha doing?" asked Bud.

The boy appeared startled for a moment, and then looked back at the computer screen, completely ignoring Bud as he started typing on his keyboard. Bud noticed the computer screen was mounted on his wheelchair, along with his keyboard.

Bud asked again, "Ah, excuse me? Hi there. Whatcha doing?" Bud moved closer to the boy, who was typing furiously.

He ignored Bud's question at first but then said, "My name is—" He stopped for a breath, exhaled, and then continued, "Peter Roberts."

Bud looked around the room. Large monitors sat on desks all around the room. Each displayed information of the expedition camp status. Bud figured the data was probably used as the screen saver. One display showing something different caught Bud's eye. It displayed the status of the information network around the world in colorful animated diagrams, illustrating data transfer. All of the workstations were empty … but very inviting, Bud thought.

"I'm Bud. How old are you?"

Aw, jeez, nothing like getting to the point, Bud thought to himself. He wasn't very good at small talk.

Peter looked over his shoulder at Bud briefly and then down at Casey and rolled his eyes. His head quickly turned back to his computer screen as his fingers danced on his keyboard on their own and said, "I'm thirteen."

Bud was impressed at Peter's typing, which got faster the longer Bud watched him. "Man, you can type fast. What are you typing?" asked Bud. Bud noticed Peter's wheelchair had large knobby wheels with chrome spokes, a large motor, a mounted computer workstation, and a control panel along the armrests. Peter let out a loud sigh as Bud continued with his barrage of questions and then finally interrupted.

"Look, ah … Bud … I'm right in the middle of Skyping with my friend, Tom. Do you mind?" Peter made a face and then sighed loudly again.

Bud shook his head. "*No problemo*; guess I'll talk to you later. Come on, Case, let's go." He knew the boy wasn't Skyping anymore, since the call had disconnected shortly after he walked into the room, but he took the hint. Bud walked out of the computer room and back into the hallway, hanging his head.

"Bud!" yelled Sara from the end of the hallway.

"Uh-oh. Dang. Case, c'mon. Case, let's go." Bud pulled Casey's collar and started jogging in the direction of Sara's voice. Casey followed.

"Where did you go, you little brat?" asked Sara. "You know Dad wants me to watch over you."

"Jeez, when did you start to care anyway? I left you a note," Bud grunted. He was really more upset at how his conversation with that boy, Peter, had gone, but he took it out on Sara anyway. "I went to the briefing with Dad, and then I thought I would take Case for a walk after it was over."

"All right, but next time, let me know where you'll be. Understand?" Sara swatted him lightly on the back of his head.

"Sure thing, serious, abusive Sara. Didn't know it mattered so much to you. After all, I was just learning my way around a little."

Bud changed his demeanor as he looked around. "It's really a cool place. You should see all the computers down the hall."

"We need to hurry. Dad wants us to go to the learning center. We're supposed to get registered today, and lucky me," she said, shaking her head, "I get to help teach the elementary class."

Bud noticed Sara was carrying a briefcase, as if she were a full-time teacher. He gave her a perplexed look. "Why you so gung ho today, anyway? One minute you're complaining, and the next—"

"Shut up, little brat. Dad asked me to help, okay?"

Bud just gave her a confused look. "C'mon, Case. I need to get you back in your kennel."

— 12 —

As Bud walked with Sara to the school section of the camp, he suddenly saw his father and Kurt walking quickly down the far end of the hallway.

"Dad!" shouted Bud.

"Shhhh," Sara said. "Dad's busy right now—keep your voice down."

Bud's father looked behind him and waved to Bud and Sara. He changed directions and immediately walked toward them, with Kurt following closely behind.

"Hi, kids. I'm getting quite the tour from Kurt," Bud's father said.

"Can I come with you?" asked Bud.

Sara gave him a frown. "You have school—" started Sara.

Kurt interrupted, "*Da*. Of course, of course he may join us, Dr. Thompson. There are no secrets here inside camp facility. Please come—come now. There is much more to see."

Bud made a face back at Sara, who turned abruptly and continued down the hallway toward the school.

Bud followed Kurt and his father into the nearby computer room. Peter was still at the computer, talking with someone.

"This is our communication gear, which connects us to the Internet via satellite," Kurt said with pride in his voice.

Bud couldn't help himself; he had to ask. "How do you provide power for all this equipment?" Bud himself was now an expert in his own right on power generation—at least for tree houses.

"Well, well, my young comrade. Excellent question. We have thirty-two power stations located outside of expedition camp. Each run by combination of diesel fuel, hydrogen fuel cells, and solar and wind power. When there's no sun during storm, we switch to engines or generate power for the station using hydrogen fuel cells."

Bud smiled and nodded. He knew all about hydrogen power, thanks to Larry. He also enjoyed impressing his father. "Where do you do the electrolysis?" asked Bud.

His father gave a surprised look.

Kurt smiled. "My, my—another very good question. As you know, through an electrolysis process, we're able to generate hydrogen. We then store in tanks surrounding expedition camp. The electrolysis is performed next to storage tanks. We melt ice, then perform electrolysis with solar and wind power. Very efficient way to store for later use."

"Well, Kurt," Bud's father said, "I must say I am very impressed. Thank you for personally overseeing all the technical details of this expedition project and pulling the teams and technology together to make it a reality. Your hard work is appreciated." Bud's father looked at his son and winked.

"Thank you," Kurt answered. "Engineers around world worked with best graduate students to devise power control and computer systems for expedition. It is quite impressive how so many people all over world worked together to get us here."

Kurt was almost glowing as he showed Bud and his father around the rest of the expedition camp. Bud could tell that Kurt took his job very seriously. "I show you Mission Control room next, although you have both seen it already, there are more features you must know; Right this way."

"Dr. Popov," Bud said, "I met a kid named Peter who was in the computer room. Do you know him?"

"*Da*, Peter is son of Dr. Roberts, department chair at UC Berkeley. Why you ask?"

"Well, I saw him with a high-tech wheelchair, talking to someone, and just wondered—"

Kurt interrupted, "It is common knowledge around camp, so no problem telling you: Peter was recently confined to wheelchair and condition has progressively gotten worse, although they say it has stabilized over last year."

"Is his father here?" asked Bud.

"No, his father made arrangements for Peter to share experience of expedition. Peter convinced father to allow him to join expedition to support computer systems that Peter is expert on. Dr. Roberts was reluctant, but made contact with me. His father felt trip would do him good. I discussed with your father, who approved his participation in expedition."

Bud looked at his father and smiled.

"He is a very talented young man," said his father. "Far more talented than many adults I know."

"How'd it happen, Dr. Popov?" asked Bud curiously.

"Bud—" started his father.

"Yes, yes, it is common question," Kurt said. He frowned and shook his head sadly before continuing. "Family was on houseboat trip during vacation three years ago. Shortly after returning home, Peter and mother became very ill. Doctors were puzzled as both Peter and mother progressively worsened. After days of testing, doctors concluded Peter and mother contracted rare form of West Nile virus when family had gone on houseboating trip. Quite tragic, really—a week later, his mother died from virus, and Peter was left with polio-like symptoms and partial paralysis."

Bud didn't know what to say as they kept walking. Having lost his own mother, he could relate to Peter's grief and thought it might explain why Peter was so reserved; after all, Bud knew how lonely being sad could feel. He pulled out the wrinkled picture of himself and his mother from his pocket and took a quick look as he followed closely behind Kurt and his father down the hallway. Now Bud really wanted to get to know Peter.

They walked down the small hallway and toward a door marked, "Mission Control—Controlled Area."

Kurt pushed the two swinging doors open. Bud did a double take; he remembered he had seen doors like this in the hospital once, but he quickly made himself think about something different.

Inside the Mission Control room, engineers were busy working at their stations and checking the systems. "All systems are looking good," said one of the system engineers over an intercom, looking over the control panels.

— 13 —

SARA SAT IN FRONT of the smiling administration clerk as Bud sneaked up behind her with Casey.

"Thank you so much, Ms. Thompson, for helping teach at our school," said the administration clerk. "Your lesson plan looks excellent, and of course you will receive teaching credit." Sara blushed and nodded.

Casey jumped up on Sara's lap and licked her face with a big gob of slobber. "Hey—yuck!" Sara jumped. "Casey!" She pushed Casey off her lap and wiped her face. "Just sign in," Sara told Bud. "You can't have Casey here."

"He'll be fine, and he'll wait outside of my classroom," Bud said with a grin. "Won't you, big boy?" Bud petted Casey's head. Bud took a seat in front of the administration clerk as Casey decided to lie down next to Bud's chair.

"Nice dog you have, Mr. Thompson," said the administration clerk. She leaned over and scratched Casey under the chin. "As long as he stays out of the classroom, I guess it's okay to have him here. Here, please take this form and fill it out before signing in."

Bud didn't waste any time. He quickly filled out the form while the administration clerk shuffled through the papers on her desk.

"Sara, you can go assist the Russian teacher in section Delta-Two with her classroom now. Bud, you're in section Delta-One. It's nice to meet you both."

"See ya, butthead," Bud said. He slapped Sara playfully on the back and ran to his classroom with Casey hobbling behind him.

Bud looked at the classroom doors. "Here it is. Delta-One," Bud said. "You stay here, Case, until class is over."

Casey whined at first, and then flopped down on the ground in frustration.

Bud slowly entered the classroom, as if he were getting into a cold swimming pool. Time stood still. All fifteen sets of eyes were on Bud, piercing him like daggers. He looked around in slow motion, feeling butterflies struggle to get out of his growling stomach. The windowless classroom was smaller than Bud was used to, with a high ceiling. Smooth white walls displayed pictures of the world and Antarctica. The teacher's huge desk stood out in the front of the classroom with a large blackboard spread across the entire front wall. Four rows of modern wooden desks filled most of the remaining room. Bud struggled to take a breath.

Somehow, the passing seconds turned into what felt like hours. Finally, Bud remembered to take deep breath. Time began to move again.

The teacher's name was neatly printed on the chalkboard in thick white chalk: Ms. Crothers. "You must be Bud," said Ms. Crothers in an Australian accent.

Bud did a double take. He looked at Ms. Crothers's long, blonde hair, which flowed down past her waist.

"Ah … yes, ma'am, I'm Bud Thompson." He turned bright red. Bud felt lost as he scanned the rest of the kids in the room.

"Welcome to our class, Bud. Please go ahead and take any open seat," said Ms. Crothers, eager to get back to her lesson plan.

Bud could feel Ms. Crothers's eyes stabbing him as he stood there, looking around for an open seat. Finally, Bud saw a face he recognized. Peter, the boy Bud had met earlier, was in the back of the room in his wheelchair. Bud saw an empty chair next to Peter and quickly made a beeline to it.

"Hi, Peter," Bud said with a half smile and an exhale of the breath he had been holding in.

Peter looked at Bud and then back at the wall where the map was hanging. Ms. Crothers had already resumed her discussion on Antarctic geology. Peter started typing on the computer keyboard attached to his wheelchair while looking at a small video display attached to the armrest.

Bud turned his attention to Ms. Crothers.

"Barometric pressure and average wind speed for the month have been very near the monthly averages at 676.6 millibars and 10.3 knots, which is 11.9 miles per hour …"

Bud looked over at Peter and whispered, "Typing on your computer again?"

Peter looked at Bud and replied quietly, "I'm e-mailing my friend at Berkeley."

"How you doing that from your wheelchair?" Bud asked with a puzzled look on his face.

Peter sat there typing for a moment and then looked up again at Bud with an annoyed look on his face. "I have a wireless Internet connection to the computer room that I hooked up last week. How else would I do it?" Peter exhaled and rolled his eyes.

Bud just looked back at the teacher and muttered under his breath, "Personally, I could think of lots of ways to do it."

Ms. Crothers pointed at the map stretched out over the front wall. "The expedition camp is located here, and the South Pole is located here ..."

— 14 —

IT WAS BRIGHT AND early when Bud ambled into the classroom while wishing he was out exploring. He had been attending the expedition school now for a few days while also trying to spend as much time as he could with his father in the Mission Control room. Today his father reminded him he had better spend some time in class before Ms. Crothers officially complained about his missed classes.

Bud dropped down into his seat as Ms. Crothers was writing on the chalkboard before class started.

"Morning."

Bud looked up to see that Peter had positioned his high-tech wheelchair next to him. It was the first time Peter had instigated conversation, and Bud was taken aback. Bud nodded, cleared his throat, and then said, "So, how long you been here? I mean, not here," he said, gesturing to the classroom, "but here. On this expedition."

Peter hesitated and then looked away.

After a long pause, Bud added, "Talking with only Casey the last few days is seriously getting old—"

"I've been here for a couple of months now," Peter interrupted, looking down.

"We just got here a few days ago. Seems like a pretty cool place. Have you explored at all?"

"Yes, I've been all over camp."

"Are there any cool places to hang out?" Bud asked as Ms. Crothers continued her preparations for class.

"Well, I do know of this one place by the drill that I like to go hang out. There are computers in there, and I've worked on a way to get onto the Internet and connect my wheelchair to the e-mail system using this high-speed wireless connection that's separate from the main connection, but I need to add more wireless routers to extend my connectivity," Peter said, still acting somewhat guarded, but clearly proud of his ability with computers.

Bud smiled; Peter was talking quickly now in computer-speak, and Bud was keeping up without a problem, as Bud had learned all about wireless Internet technology when he was working with Larry at the Space Center.

Bud wanted to get to know Peter, so he played along, pretending not to fully understand. But Peter just kept going on and on, and it was starting to drive Bud crazy. Finally, Bud grew tired of this game.

Bud let it all out at once: "Hey, let's go there after school today. I need to connect my XG phone to the local wifi link, so I can e-mail my friends back home. I've also queued up a series of tweets I want to send out. Before we came here, I wrote an app that will link my phone to any secure wifi link within the expedition to piggyback on the expedition's Internet traffic in order to send and receive e-mail using the expedition's backup satellite uplink. My phone can reroute its e-mail and other communication over multiple links simultaneously to guarantee delivery when the main comm link has no bandwidth." Bud took a breath and then added, "Even from the bottom of the world."

Bud smiled, proud that he had just completely surprised Peter with his knowledge.

Peter's mouth dropped open as he stared at Bud with a shocked, yet impressed, expression. Their friendship was now official.

Ms. Crothers started the class, and the morning went by quickly for Bud. The more Peter loosened up, the more Bud felt as if he might actually have someone to hang out with around the expedition camp. But the real motivator for Bud was Peter's knowledge of all the cool technology around the camp and how to use it.

Although … there's something else we have in common. But Bud didn't want to bring that up.

— 15 —

OVER THE NEXT COUPLE of weeks, Peter and Bud sat next to each other in the classroom and were nearly inseparable outside of class. When they first started exploring the expedition camp, Bud kept staring at Peter's wheelchair. But once Bud got to know Peter better, the wheelchair just became a way for Peter to get around, although Bud thought the wheelchair was pretty darn cool, with its high-tech components allowing it to connect to everything around the expedition camp.

Bud added a few additional "green-fuel technology features," as Larry would say, to the wheelchair with equipment he had brought with him to the camp. This included high-powered battery chargers in order to help the wheelchair's batteries keep up with all of Peter's electronic gadgets. Another device Bud added was a wind-power generator and propeller that generated power whenever Peter moved his wheelchair, recharging the wheelchair's batteries.

Bud had brought a half a dozen fuel cells that Larry had given him, tucked away in his oversized backpack. He showed Peter how to use electrolysis to collect hydrogen, which they placed in empty metal containers secured to the bottom of the wheelchair. These were used as fuel for the additional fuel cells Bud added, along with a portable recharging station for two smartphones. Larry had given him a dozen of the phones to play with, and Bud had brought them all.

Bud secured the fuel cells on the back of the wheelchair in a thin, plastic suitcase he had found, along with all the wiring and other electronic parts to provide power wherever Peter needed it. Peter's wheelchair had turned into a wind- and water-powered mobile Internet communication station. A small makeshift antenna was positioned on top of the suitcase, which Bud connected to a wireless access point.

During lunchtime, Bud stood on the back of the wheelchair while Peter gave him rides around the classroom area and adjoining hallways. Bud thought that was pretty exciting, since the wheelchair had much more acceleration now thanks to their recent modifications. Bud rode around with his sunglasses on, looking pretty cool in a geeky sort of way.

After Ms. Crothers let the class out on one particular school day, Bud asked, "How 'bout we go to the computer room?" His voice was full of excitement. "I want to send some e-mail."

"Okay, but I need to check in with my guardian first," Peter said.

"Guardian?" Bud looked surprised; Peter hadn't mentioned a guardian before.

"Yeah, my father couldn't come on the expedition. They would only let me come if I had a guardian to help me around this place."

"So why did you come here anyway?"

Peter's face lit up as they cruised slowly out of the classroom with Bud riding on the back of the wheelchair and Casey, who had been waiting quietly outside the classroom, hobbling closely behind. Peter talked really fast when he drove his wheelchair around. "Well, I really love computers, and this place has the coolest system in the world. It is totally high tech and has multiple high-bandwidth connections with multiple clusters, and—"

Bud interrupted, "Wait a minute. Can you stop here? I need to talk to my sister."

Peter stopped abruptly at Sara's classroom. Bud jumped off the wheelchair and ran into the classroom. The entire class turned around and looked at him as he entered. Bud had forgotten he still had his sunglasses on, but when he remembered, he felt pretty cool.

"Tell Dad if you see him later that I'll be exploring the camp with Peter, okay?"

Sara just looked at Bud and gave him a nod.

Bud ran out of the classroom and jumped on the back of Peter's wheelchair as Peter took off. They cruised over to Peter's living quarters and told his guardian where they were going. Bud quickly figured out that his guardian was really a nurse, but he didn't say anything to Peter.

They drove down the long hallway toward the computer room. Casey loped along behind them, trying to keep up, slobbering all over the hallway and occasionally barking in an attempt to slow the boys down.

They turned a corner sharply. "How long you been cruisin' in this chair?" Bud asked.

"For about three years now. They say I have some sort of muscle thing where my muscles get progressively weaker. I got something called West Nile virus when I was on a vacation with my family. It's a long story ... but don't worry, it's not contagious," Peter said while navigating his wheelchair quickly around another corner.

Bud nodded as if this were all news to him. Although Kurt had already told him, Bud had decided just to pretend that he was hearing the information for the first time.

"Here's the place I was telling you about." Peter stopped suddenly, almost throwing Bud off the back of the wheelchair. "They're drilling right over there in that room."

Peter had taken Bud to the center of the facility, where the drilling was in full operation. From a computer center adjacent to the drilling room, the live Internet connection was beamed via satellite uplink to the rest of the world. Team members busily checked gauges and monitors throughout the room. No one noticed Bud and Peter as they entered the computer center.

"Let's use this one," Peter said as he positioned his wheelchair in front of a computer monitor.

Peter logged onto the computer and began checking his e-mail with Bud looking over his shoulder. He had received an e-mail. It read,

Hey, Peter,

How's it going at the bottom of the world? We're monitoring things back here in the lab. Sure is exciting. But not really much to do until the probe breaks through the ice. Well, got to go. Just wanted to say hello. Hope all is well. Oh yeah, your father is sure proud of you and misses you, too, but you know how he is about e-mailing …

Later,

T

"Who's T?" Bud asked.

"He's one of my father's students—Tom Sutton. He got his degree before he was eighteen, and now he's in graduate school, working on computers. He's helping run a really cool computer center that my father is in charge of and is helping with data analysis for the expedition. Tom's really cool and treats me like I'm one of his classmates. He taught me a ton about computers."

Peter quickly replied to Tom's e-mail.

Tom,
Doing good. Staying busy. Tell Dad I miss him, too.
TTFN,
Peter

"What does TTFN mean?" Bud asked.

"Ta-a for now," replied Peter with a half smile.

Bud rolled his eyes.

"What's your father doing for the expedition at Berkeley?"

"He's in charge of the environmental computer systems."

"Huh? Environmental? What do those computers do?"

"They have a dedicated Internet connection to the expedition with three computer systems. Those systems will preprocess the data we collect from the probe once the drill gets down to the lake and the probe starts collecting information. I get to help on this end when they activate the probe."

Bud was impressed. "Really? You get to help?"

Peter nodded. "I get to monitor the probe sensor computer station in Mission Control. Hey, maybe you can help, too."

"What do the computers—"

Before Bud could finish his question, Peter replied, "One computer will analyze the environmental telemetry from the probe, one computer will process the images received from the live video camera on the probe, and one computer will run experiments on the data. I'm sure your dad will let you help me. There's a lot to monitor," Peter said with excitement.

zzzzzzEEEEEeeeee. A high-pitched squealing noise came from the drilling room, and it was getting louder.

"Hey, let's check it out," Bud said.

"Hop on." Peter drove his wheelchair into the hallway.

People were moving in every direction when the boys entered the Mission Control room. A group of scientists were engaged in excited discussion as they moved quickly through the hall.

Bud and Peter looked to where the drilling was going on. The drilling room was surrounded by reinforced, clear plastic walls. They moved out of the way as team members rushed down the hallway, talking as they walked.

"Hey, mate, we're getting close now," one of the team members remarked to another team member in an Australian accent. "We'd best notify Mr. Popov pronto."

"Let's go find my dad," Bud said.

They made a right turn and headed toward Mission Control.

— 16 —

BUD'S FATHER WAS ENGAGED in conversation with an engineer when the boys arrived at Mission Control.

Peter took his position within the busy room. A large label on the workstation where he sat in his wheelchair displayed the words "probe telemetry."

Bud sat close to Peter, looking over his shoulder as he typed like a madman on the computer. "You're the world's fastest typist. What are you typing, anyway?"

Peter kept typing while he looked at Bud. "I need to complete the self-tests to make sure the probe is ready to go on this end. That way I can pass on the data points to Tom to finish setting up their computers."

"How do you type without looking at the keyboard? You're amazing." Bud stared down at Peter's fingers, which were flying across the keyboard, and then back up at Peter, who was looking at him and smiling.

"Practice."

Bud's father walked up to Bud and Peter. "Hi, boys. I see Peter is showing you what our probe does."

"It's amazing," Bud said. "The probe generates a ton of information. Hard to believe the information is placed on the Internet once it is received from below. That's way cool."

"Yes, son. The days of depending on CNN for updates are in the past … although we do try to take a look at some of the technical data before it's broadcast over the Internet for everyone to see."

"Really? Why?" asked Bud.

"Well, let's just say that there are some who want to make sure no sensitive data goes on the Internet, since the Internet is used worldwide. Just think of it this way: people around the world will be able to access the expedition website and watch us in their pajamas from the comfort of their nicely heated homes thousands of miles away—"

Kurt walked up to Bud's father, interrupting him. "Comrade, good news. Dr. Roberts called and confirmed Berkeley computer center up and running. They online and receive real-time test telemetry data from our Internet broadcast."

Bud's father gave Kurt a quick nod. "Thanks, Kurt. Peter seems to have everything ready to go on this end, too. We'll need their computer horsepower to run the experiments."

"Press waits. Wants to know when we have first press conference," Kurt said with an impatient exhale of breath.

"Press?" asked Bud.

"Yes," Bud's father said. "I need to keep them informed as to our status—something to do with the importance of keeping public opinion high about the expedition. I suppose it's a good thing."

Kurt left abruptly, and Bud's father started to leave as well when Bud grabbed his arm. "Can I help Peter with the probe? After all, I am an intern at the Space Center."

"Sure, sure, but don't get in Peter's way. He has a—"

Peter interrupted as he kept typing at supersonic speed. "It's not a problem, Dr. Thompson. I'll show Bud how the computer system works, and he can help me."

"Okay, boys, but you can only come in here during operations when you can be supervised." Bud's father paused as he gave Bud a serious look that quickly changed to a smile. "We're making history with this expedition, and I am glad you're both part of it."

Bud looked around the room as his father walked away. "Man, there sure are a lot of people in here."

"Intern?" Peter mused. "You're an intern at the Space Center?"

"Yeah, they wanted me to help with some of the projects there," Bud said, beaming.

Peter gave Bud a nod. "You didn't … I mean, why didn't you tell me that before?" Peter asked.

"You never asked," Bud said with a Cheshire-cat smile. After all, he couldn't resist putting Peter in his place occasionally, even if he had become a good friend.

"Very cool," Peter said with admiration.

17

THE DAY THE EXPEDITION team had been working toward had finally arrived. Bud's stomach fluttered with excitement as he finished his breakfast cereal alongside his dad.

"Good luck today, Dad," Sara said, still in her bathrobe. "Today's the big day, isn't it?"

"Thanks. Sure is. Today's the day I've been looking forward to since I saw that first satellite image months ago back at the Space Center."

Bud swallowed with a gulp and then garbled, "You mean the first image we both saw at the Space Center, right, Dad?" Bud nearly choked on his food.

His father nodded. "That's right, Bud. You're absolutely right. The satellite image we saw." He took a loud sip of his hot coffee as he stood. "How is your class going at school?" he said to Sara.

"Okay. They have me teaching English and math now."

"That's great, honey."

"I guess," said Sara. "Not much else to do around here."

"We better go, Bud. Peter is probably already there and waiting for your help."

"Did you—" started Bud.

"Yes, I talked with Ms. Crothers yesterday."

"Thanks, Dad." Bud pushed his chair away from the table, rushing out of the door behind his father. "Today's going to be wicked cool, Dad."

"Wicked?"

"Really cool. It means really cool." Bud rolled his eyes.

"Oh, okay. Yes, today will be wicked cool," Bud's father agreed.

Bud shook his head and raised his eyebrows. "Do you think we'll find something in the lake once the probe gets there?"

"No idea. Right now, I'm just thinking about the data, the research around the world, and the research centers that will be analyzing the data collected from the probe." Bud's father paused as he looked at Bud. "But who knows? Maybe we will find something that is, like you said, uh, wicked cool." They both laughed.

Bud and his father arrived at the Mission Control room shortly after 6:00 a.m. The core team was already at their stations, doing system checks, and Peter was positioned at the probe computer workstation, typing like a madman already.

Kurt greeted Bud's father with an out-of-character handshake. "Good morning, comrade. Good morning, Mr. Bud. All systems go. Ready to commence final countdown on your mark, comrade," Kurt said in a calm, cool, distinctly Russian tone as he looked at Bud's father.

Bud sat down in the open chair next to Peter and looked around the room. He put on a headset that allowed him to tune to different webcam channels, allowing him to talk to and listen in on any computer lab around the world that was participating in the expedition.

"Mornin'," Bud said to Peter, covering his microphone and trying to act calm and cool. "Today's gonna be a pretty exciting day."

Peter nodded without looking at Bud.

Data on the main screen was appearing in four quadrants. Internet connectivity statuses and e-mail messages were scrolling in one quadrant; the video cam was showing a black image in another; the environmental data was in another; and the last quadrant showed the probe's positioning information.

Bud could hear his father greet the team: "Good morning, ladies and gentlemen. Today is the day we have all been working toward; we're finally ready to insert the probe. With hard work and a little luck, we're a couple of days from reaching a body of water that has not been exposed to our environment for thousands, if not even millions, of years …"

Bud was distracted by all the information he saw around the room. He looked closely at the computer screen directly in front of him and listened as his father checked in with the person at each computer station to make sure they were ready. Bud thought it was sort of a redundant process, especially since all the systems showed up on his monitor with a green "Go" next to each station leader's name, but Peter told him it gave each key scientist a chance to verbally delay the start of the mission if they saw a problem.

"Internet?"

"Ready 1."

"Environmental?"

"Ready 2."

"Mechanical?"

"Ready 3."

"Electrical?"

"Ready 4."

"Fuel?"

"Ready 5."

"Probe?"

After a pause, Peter elbowed Bud, who realized it was his turn. Bud looked down at his screen with all green readings and said, "Ready 6."

Bud smiled.

The checks continued.

"Depth?"

"Ready 7."

"Research centers?"

"Ready 8."

"Mission coordinator?"

"All systems go." Everything was ready to start.

"Ladies and gentlemen," Bud's father said, "let's begin the countdown. T minus ten seconds on my mark."

Bud continued to look around the room. The entire team was watching his father and listening for the final countdown command. Bud's heart pounded with anticipation.

"Commence final countdown, mark," Bud's father said with authority.

The large clock on the display wall showed the countdown time. 10 … 9 … 8 … 7 … 6 … 5 …

The drilling engines roared louder.

… 4 … 3 … 2 … 1 … 0.

"Dr. Thompson, probe insertion has commenced," Kurt said. "Repeat, probe insertion is now active." The clock overhead began to show positive time: 1 … 2 … 3 … 4 …

The large monitor began showing real-time data. None of the information quadrants meant anything to Bud except for the probe depth and drilling status. It showed the speed of the drill and the current depth. The probe insertion started somewhat slowly as hot, sterile water was sprayed at super high speed and vacuumed out just as quickly. Bud watched his screen as a video started of the sterile water rushing down the drilling arm, making a swooshing sound he could hear in the control room.

"What happens when the water hits the ice, Peter?" Bud asked.

"It's recycled back to the surface and sterilized. The hot water is then shot back down to the drill and impacts the ice again. The excess water sprays out one mile away from the expedition site." Peter paused, taking a breath and looking at a couple of numbers on his computer screen, and then continued. "At this rate, it will take the probe forty-eight hours to come within ten feet of the lake. Not much excitement will happen until then. But we'll monitor progress closely to ensure the drilling maintains proper speed parameters."

Bud could see video from computer rooms around the world. He saw one video stream marked "UC Berkeley— Dr. Roberts—Channel 17." Bud selected channel 17. A video began to stream from the UC Berkeley computer lab to Bud's computer screen. In the video image, a number of people could be seen working in the UC Berkeley computer lab. Bud pointed to his screen. "Hey, is this your dad's lab?"

Peter nodded.

Bud saw a young-looking student in the Berkeley computer lab on the video. The student was dialing a speakerphone in the lab. Bud noticed the clock in the lab; it was late in the evening at Berkeley due to the time difference. Bud could see and hear everything going on in the Berkeley computer lab.

"Roberts here," said the voice over the speakerphone.

"Hi, Dr. Roberts. This is Tom. Probe insertion has started and is looking good at this point."

"Great, Tom. Let me know if any problems occur. Let's plan on pulling an all-nighter when the preparations for final ice breakthrough begin."

"Sure thing, Dr. Roberts."

"Tom, pizza's here," said one of the undergrads from across the room.

Bud took off his headset and tapped on Peter's shoulder. "Peter, check out channel 17. Is that the Tom you were talking about?"

Peter adjusted his headset, tuned into channel 17, and watched it for a few seconds on his computer screen. "Yep, that's him." Peter typed a few things on his computer.

Hey, Tom, we can see you from the expedition camp.

Bud watched Tom look more closely at the computer monitors in his lab that showed the Mission Control room. Bud smiled when Tom finally noticed Bud and Peter waving to him. "Hey, Peter! Who's the kid next to you?" Tom said.

"He's Dr. Thompson's son, Bud, and he's helping me with the probe."

"Hi, Bud. Nice to meet you. Looks like our historic breakthrough will occur soon. I need to get back to monitoring on our end. Nice to see you, Peter, and nice meeting you, Bud." Tom abruptly disconnected the channel on his end.

Bud remembered he needed to feed Casey and take him for a walk. He reluctantly left Mission Control without disturbing Peter. He was busy reviewing the probe data.

$=$ 18 $=$

THE NEXT COUPLE OF days went by quickly. Bud skipped school and went directly to the Mission Control room to work closely with Peter to learn the system.

When Bud came into the Mission Control room on one such busy day, he saw his father on the other side of the room, but he looked busy, so Bud sat down next to Peter. Peter was hard at work already.

"You look tired," Bud said.

"Yeah, I had to work another all-nighter."

"How does everything look?"

"Making some final adjustments," Peter answered. "Want to make sure this thing is going to work without any problems."

Bud's father made an announcement over the intercom: "Okay, folks, this is what we have all come here to see. Let's push the probe through the last ten feet of the ice."

Peter started typing faster than ever. "Looks like you arrived just in time," Peter said. The large display showed a visual representation of the probe's position relative to the lake. Numbers and measurements surrounded the visual image. "Here, use this pen to write down the data points and the time on the sheet when they change."

Bud looked closely at his computer screen, which showed all the data points in green. "This is wicked cool," Bud said as he poised his pen above the paper to write down the data.

Kurt called out the final countdown. "Five feet, four feet, three feet, two feet, one foot … breakthrough! We have probe insertion." The room filled with cheers and applause.

"Prepare for probe telemetry," Kurt said, watching the large displays at the front of the room.

Peter responded like a seasoned professional; even Bud was impressed. "The probe is nearing the lake. Prepare for telemetry in two minutes," Peter said.

Bud heard his father over the intercom again. "Let's prepare the uplink to the Internet. There is a whole world out there waiting to receive the information as we collect it."

Bud saw Peter turn to channel 17, so he did the same.

"Dad," Peter said, "they've broken through the ice with the probe. You should begin receiving probe telemetry shortly."

"Great, son," said Dr. Roberts. "We'll triple check our systems on this end to make sure everything is operational."

— 19 —

BUD AND PETER CONTINUED working in the control room, monitoring the status of the probe. "All systems are go, Dr. Thompson," Peter said. "We're receiving telemetry now. The telemetry is also being transmitted to the Internet. We will broadcast the video feed to the Internet in one minute. The probe should be in the lake"— Peter paused, confirming the readings on his computer screen—"now."

Bud looked around the room. Everyone in the room seemed to be, at most, three inches from their computer screens, observing the readings.

"What the heck?" Peter said with a frown. "Bud, check your readings—do you see what I see?"

"Looks like we have a malfunction. The probe is reading 65 degrees Fahrenheit, which is expected, but these other readings don't make sense," Bud said. "How can—"

Peter interrupted. "Dr. Thompson, look at these readings. They're showing high ... ah ... oxygen levels."

"Do we have probe webcam online yet?" barked Kurt.

"No, sir," said a team member. "We're trying to adjust it locally first … here and here … okay, it is now online. Probe webcam activated. Video coming into only the Mission Control room now. Wait, what the …"

Bud looked up at the large display in the front of the room along with most of the team; confused whispers spread like wildfire throughout the room. The previous image on the projection screen of the probe's position had been replaced with a full-screen video image from the probe. Where they had expected to see a dark underwater image to be displayed, a blurred, light-green image with shimmering white floating particles and red and blue light streaks displayed on the monitor.

"Kurt, do we have a malfunction? How can there be light and oxygen down there, and why the hell aren't we in water?" asked Bud's father. "Please adjust the probe webcam to the downward position. Position it to a point directly below its present position."

The probe was now scanning from the left and moving slowly down and to the right. Different images were beginning to appear in a purplish hue that radiated off the towering rock material surrounding the lake. Then, from around the lake below came blurs in the shapes of large, glowing, dark-yellow branches, white grasses, streaks of light, and what appeared to be incredibly huge leaves.

"Adjust the focus," demanded Bud's father.

"Huh?" Kurt said. "Looks like, like … jungle … incredible…"

Bud's father began to shout out commands. A sinking feeling overcame Bud. The room filled with action as the team members checked and double-checked their data and reported readings. Discussion broke out among the team members. No one was watching the video display except for Bud. Peter was also distracted.

Suddenly Bud saw some sort of creature that appeared to be walking in the blurred, glowing jungle far below. The image appeared for only two seconds and then disappeared.

"Peter! Dad, did you see that?"

"Bud, we're a little busy here. We all see that," Bud's father said.

"No, Dad, I mean that very large thing walking in the jungle."

"What?" Bud's father looked up at the image, but nothing in it was walking. "Bud, please."

"But seriously. I saw something walking." Bud turned to Peter. "You saw it, right?"

Peter shook his head.

"Did anyone see any movement in the image?" Bud's father asked the team in the Mission Control room.

The team members shook their heads and looked at Bud as if he were starting to lose it.

"Sorry, son. You must have seen some sort of visual anomaly," Bud's father said.

"I know I saw something very, very big," Bud said with intensity in his eyes.

Bud's father looked back at his computer screen and studied the data.

Bud refused to take his eyes off the screen, certain he had seen something more than just a jungle.

"Continue the insertion of the probe," Bud's father said. "Can someone tell me what in the world we're looking at down there?"

"The temperature is now reading 68 degrees Fahrenheit and climbing, the lower we insert the probe," Peter said.

"We're now at thirty feet below the ice breakthrough. The oxygen levels continue to go higher still."

"Let's proceed until we find the bottom of whatever we have encountered here," Bud's father said.

Images of a vast jungle area were coming in more clearly. The area surrounded a dark mass that Bud thought was the lake. But there were no images of anything walking below.

"We're at fifty feet past the ice breakthrough point, sir," reported Peter. "Temperature is reading 70 degrees Fahrenheit. Now we're at one thousand feet … temperature is 74 degrees; two thousand seventy feet, 76 degrees; four thousand seventy-nine feet, 77 degrees."

"We have reached what appears to be lake," reported Kurt. "Fresh water with average sodium chloride content."

The room had become very quiet. Everyone was looking at Bud's father for a reaction. He began pacing back and forth while looking at the monitors.

Bud knew his father had been surprised and was trying to figure out what to do. After all, Bud had seen his father pace many times when he was getting in trouble for one thing or another. Bud knew something was wrong—very wrong.

"Well, folks, let's begin studying the data here. I want to know more about what we're seeing," Bud's father said. "We'll need to hold a press conference soon."

Peter turned to Bud and said, "Guess the world will be asking questions about what we just discovered."

"Heck, I want to know what I saw," Bud said.

"It would have to be pretty darn big to see more than four thousand feet away. Maybe you just saw—" Peter started.

"I know I saw some sort of thing walking down there," Bud insisted.

— 20 —

Bud could tell as he watched channel 17 that Peter's father was very excited about the video received at the UC Berkeley laboratory. Dr. Roberts's voice was even trembling as he studied the incoming telemetry with Tom. "This is absolutely unbelievable. It looks like there is enough oxygen for life to exist down there. These telemetry readings are incredible. A jungle? How can that be? And light?"

Bud watched as Dr. Roberts and Tom looked closely at the computer monitors on the display screen.

The webcast from the URA expedition had just started arriving at the remote sites. The probe webcam began a 360-degree rotation and scanned a circle below. The video showed large, dark leaves and what appeared to be huge trees and light-colored grasses adjacent to the dark lake. Flashes of multicolored light reflected off everything in the image. Probe telemetry data scrolled adjacent to the video images on the computer screen.

Bud and Peter reviewed the same video on their individual screens. "Look. You can almost see movement in what looks to be a jungle," Peter said. "There must be a slight breeze moving through the jungle. This is amazing!"

The streaming video images were replaced with images of an empty briefing room podium. A circular URA Expedition graphic was prominently displayed on the front of the empty podium.

Bud's father made an announcement over the intercom. "Dr. Roberts, we're going to the press conference. We're on our way now. Please notify the other remote sites ASAP that the press conference will be on channel 99."

"Understood," Dr. Roberts said.

Bud turned to channel 99 to listen to his father's press conference.

Peter typed furiously on the computer, checking and rechecking the readings.

"Why won't my dad believe me?" Bud said. "I did see something walking down there."

"It's easy to get confused," Peter said as he kept typing.

Bud changed the channel to 99-2 to get a view of the press members who would be watching his father in the pressroom. "The room is completely packed," Bud said. "Why are there so many of them?"

"I guess every country insisted on having a press rep or two," Peter said.

"That's a lot of reporters who will be watching my dad," replied Bud.

"It sure is," Peter agreed. "Not to mention the millions of people who will be watching the webcast."

All the remote monitoring stations were being displayed in numerous video boxes on the large screen in the front of the Mission Control room. Every display showed an image of the empty podium where Bud's father would soon speak. The press had assembled and now anxiously awaited the briefing.

"Man, word sure spreads fast around this place," Bud said. "Look at this—more people are packing into the room."

Bud was determined to find out more about the image he had seen when no one else was looking. He tried to replay the video in a second display box on his screen, but he couldn't. "Peter, why can't I replay the start of the video?"

"Not sure. Must have had a recording glitch that delayed the recording for the first few minutes of the video."

Bud switched back to channel 99 with some frustration. Kurt and his father were now both standing at the podium, getting ready to speak. Bud's father adjusted the microphone.

Peter stopped what he was doing and looked over to Bud's screen to watch the webcast.

"Good evening," Bud's father greeted the press. "This morning we broke through the ice with the probe as scheduled, at approximately 0835. We expected to enter the lake water shortly after ice breakthrough. But instead, we appear to have made a historical discovery. There appears to be 4,079 feet of empty space between the ice breakthrough point and the lake. We also appear to have discovered what looks to be tropical vegetation in the environment surrounding the Antarctic lake. The temperature is 77 degrees Fahrenheit with a slight three-miles-per-hour wind from the northeast. And the humidity is an amazing 90 percent." Bud's father paused for a moment.

The press could not contain their excitement. The noise of their chatter blasted into Bud's ears, and he turned the volume down slightly.

Questions came all at once from around the room. "How can there be light down there?" "Is there animal life?" "How can there be wind?" "Are there—"

Kurt pounded his hand on the podium and raised his voice. Some of the words came out in Russian. "Ladies, gentlemen—please, please, give Dr. Thompson a moment to explain!"

"Man, that shut them up," Bud said as the pressroom went silent. He turned the volume back up.

Bud's father took off his glasses and wiped his face.

"Oh, boy, that's not a good sign," Bud said as he watched his father. "He looks pretty nervous."

"Well, many unanswered questions remain," Bud's father said. "Here's where we're at at the moment—"

One of the press members interrupted, "How can light get through two miles of ice?"

Bud's father continued without skipping a beat. "We presently have no idea how light could make its way through two miles of ice, nor do we know how there could be enough light down there to sustain what appears to be organic plant life. The light readings suggest wavelengths of about 10 percent 475 nanometers and about 90 percent 670 nanometers. Excuse me, I'm sorry—that refers to blue and red light wavelengths that are known to support photosynthesis. In other words, those wavelengths would allow plants to grow ..."

"See, there is life down there," remarked Bud.

Peter shrugged and continued watching.

"... The resulting light purplish hue could suggest a possible mineral-oriented light source, such as some sort of crystal silicon carbide, known as carborundum—that is, a compound of silicon and carbon commonly referred to as SiC. It occurs in nature as the very rare mineral moissanite, which we have found in meteorites and corundum deposits. It would then need some sort of electrical energy to generate light in a way similar to how the latest light-emitting diode lamps work."

"What's a light-emitting diode?" someone yelled.

"Oh, ah, light-emitting diodes, or LEDs, are ... well, think of them as very small lightbulbs that fit onto an electrical circuit. But they are different from lightbulbs, since they don't require a filament and they don't get hot. They basically use semiconductor material, such as moissanite—"

"Meteorites? There are meteorites down there? Generating light? Are there aliens?"

Bud looked at Peter again. "Well, no one believes me, but I'm pretty sure I saw some sort of glowing alien walking down there!"

Peter ignored him.

Bud's father continued, "Please. Please, folks, let's not get carried away. It is scientifically possible that light could be generated from mineral sources, biological sources, or both. It has long been known since the experiments of H. J. Rounds, whose experiment known as the cat's whisker detector ..."

"Oh, boy, the press is going to be confused by that one," Peter said. The press roared as quickly as Peter finished his sentence.

"Cats? There are cats down there?" yelled a press member.

"No, no, no, I'm sorry. Please give me a chance to explain. In 1907, H. J. Rounds discovered that a crystal of carborundum gave off yellow light when he applied a voltage source to it using a wire. The wire is affectionately known as the cat whisker."

"That's pretty impressive," Peter said.

"What do you mean?" Bud asked.

"That your father knows so much about history."

"Yeah, he surprises me all the time," Bud said.

Bud's father continued, "But this would mean there is some sort of electrical power source causing the crystal to glow, and we have no idea how that could happen or if it is even possible to generate enough light from that alone to support organic plant life. However, there may be other reasons there is enough light down there to enable organic plant life. Interestingly enough, while we think it is rare on Earth, silicon barbide is a mineral that is amazingly common in space. But please, folks, we will need time to investigate these discoveries before we start jumping to premature conclusions, and I am sorry if my explanation has caused some confusion." Bud's father nodded to Kurt to continue.

"Probe telemetry suggests ice above lake region shaped in massive ice dome surrounded by mountains," Kurt said. "Dome apparently has supported massive greenhouse effect over entire lake biosphere, and readings show enough humidity to support periodic rain."

The press yelled again. "Rain? What? It rains down there?"

Kurt continued, "Excuse, excuse, please. We speculates at this time."

"Did you ever notice Kurt sounds more Russian when he gets stressed?" Bud said.

"He definitely looks stressed," Peter said. "More than your father."

"Thank you, Kurt," Bud's father said. "Yes, there is a possibility it rains enough to support the organic plant life surrounding the lake. The probe readings suggest a land region extending over 10 kilometers or 6.2 miles from the lake in all directions, supporting a variety of plant life. Folks, for reasons unknown at this time, life appears to have developed down there."

The press roared louder now with even more questions. "Are there animals down there?" "Dinosaurs?" "Are there people?"

Bud's father continued, "Please, folks. We don't know any more at this time. We will confer with the URA members and members from the Scientific Committee on Antarctica Research, also known as SCAR, to determine our next plan of action. This is absolutely the most incredible discovery of our time, and we want to make sure that any actions we take today will not destroy whatever environment has evolved below over thousands, if not millions, of years. That's all for now. Thank you."

Bud's father ended his briefing, and the screen went blank.

"That went better than I expected," Bud said. "Who the heck would have ever thought life could have existed down there?"

"Well, I guess life has a way of surviving and evolving in the most difficult of environments," Peter said, sounding quite scholarly.

"Yeah, but I still don't get it," Bud said. "How could there be enough light down there to sustain life?"

Kurt and his father walked into the Mission Control room near where Bud and Peter were sitting.

"Kurt, do we have the water filtration system set up?" Bud's father asked.

"Yes, comrade, it is ready," Kurt said. "We have each of four filters online, and probe positioned slightly below lake surface."

"How long will it take to get a complete water sample?"

"About hour to filter fifty gallons of lake water."

"All right. I want all the excess lake water we filter stored as well. Labs around the world will want to analyze it."

"*Da*. I get team started on it immediately."

"Good. Call me when it's done," Bud's father said. "I need to start preparing for what could be a very long series of meetings." He looked over to where Bud and Peter were sitting. "Bud, why don't you go with Kurt, and he can show you how his filtration system works. Peter has a great deal of work to do."

"Sure thing, Dad!" Bud said.

Kurt looked down at Bud with a frown. "Come with me."

— 21 —

Bud watched the monitors curiously as the team prepared the water filtration equipment within the filtration room. The filtration system had been installed in the center of the room with a large pipe connecting to the probe far below.

"So that filter will test water from the lake?" asked Bud.

"*Da*. Water from lake pumped through probe into pipe and to filtration system," responded Kurt without looking at Bud.

"Sir, now 3 meters, or almost 10 feet, below the lake surface," said a team member.

"Hold, please. Is filtration system online?" asked Kurt.

"Yes, sir. Each of the four filters is online—"

"How do these filters work?" asked Bud, interrupting Kurt.

Kurt gave Bud an annoyed look and replied, "The filtration system uses four filters designed large enough to capture different size bacteria and viruses, if present. Filters placed in sterilized containers and will be removed and froze for shipment to lab back in US to analyze collected materials."

"Bacteria and viruses?" asked Bud.

"In typical milliliter of seawater anywhere in world, we typically expect to collect approximately one million bacteria and ten million viruses with this system," Kurt said. "It proves life diverse all around world, since bacteria and viruses very common. Filter one remove all life above 10 microns, filter two remove all life bigger than 4 microns, filter three remove all life bigger than .9 microns, and filter four remove life bigger than .1 microns."

"What's a micron?" Bud whispered to a young scientist standing next him.

"Think of it this way," the scientist whispered. ".1 micron is nearly 1,000 times thinner than a human hair."

Bud pulled one of his hairs and looked at it. He was still confused about how this contraption worked. "You mean each filter can capture different-sized creatures if they're in the lake?" asked Bud.

"*Da*, that is what I said."

Bud looked at the scientist next to him and rolled his eyes. The scientist just ignored him.

"Engage pump," commanded Kurt harshly.

The low-pitched sound pulsated slowly as it sucked water up from the lake and into the filters. Kurt walked over to the filters and monitored the gauge on the front of each of the four cylinders. The gauge, color-coded green, yellow, and red, displayed the pressure within each cylinder.

"What do the different colors mean?" asked Bud.

Kurt let out a loud sigh and gave a look to the young scientist next to Bud, who answered him.

"Colors? Well, yellow means the filter is completely saturated and ready for removal, and red indicates anomaly—ah, that means a problem occurred," said the young scientist to Bud.

Bud nodded. He was starting to understand now how this system worked. He followed the pipe with his eyes from where it entered the filtration room to the filtration system and then looked at the gauges.

"Where is the water now?" Bud asked the young scientist next to him.

"It is almost here. Ten more seconds," whispered the team member.

The needles on the gauges started moving. The needles moved from green to just inside the yellow as the pump began to make a low-pitched humming sound. Suddenly, all gauges went to red, and the low-pitched humming sound changed to a deafening high-pitched screech. Everyone in the room covered their ears, and the sound vibrated in Bud's head.

Three technicians ran to the filtration system as Bud jumped out of the way.

"Sir, we need to turn it off—now!" a team member yelled. "Pressure is building quickly."

"Turn off now!" Kurt yelled back, along with a few choice Russian swear words.

Once the red button was pressed, the high-pitched screech slowly faded. Without moving his eyes from the cylinders, Bud took a breath when he realized he was holding it in.

"Open first cylinder. We see what have," Kurt said urgently.

A technician unlatched the metal buckle securing the top of the metal cylinder and then grabbed the top with both hands. He grunted as he worked hard, trying to turn it to get it to open.

Without warning, it gave way and opened all at once, with water bursting all over the floor in a large splash— along with at least a hundred small, minnow-like fish, each with eyes almost as wide as its body, flapping around loudly on the floor of the filtration room.

But Bud wasn't looking at the minnow-sized fish. He was staring at the one large, long-nosed, thick-bodied fish with huge eyes and two-inch needle teeth jaggedly arranged under its long nose.

Bud jumped backward as the large fish flapped around the floor with its mouth opening and closing like a bear trap as it tried unsuccessfully to pass water over its exposed gills.

"Holy guacamole, that fish is ugly!" Bud said.

"Get back—" said one technician as the technicians ran for cover away from the puddle of flapping fish.

Bud moved slowly toward the smaller fish on the floor. He crouched down and picked up one with two fingers, studying it. He looked at it closely, with his nose about four inches from the creature.

Kurt saw Bud touching the creature.

"Please do not touch," started Kurt. "We do not know what—"

Suddenly the fish jerked, and Bud jumped as the little creature shot from Bud's two fingers and fell to the floor, flopping around wildly.

Bud stumbled backward, nearly falling over as he tried to move away.

"I knew it," Bud said. "Creatures of the lake. Wicked cool!" Bud loved it when he was right ... although, as he looked closely at the large fish's jagged teeth, he wasn't completely sure that was a good thing at the moment.

Bud glanced over at Kurt, who looked completely stressed.

"Please, everyone, back away from spill. Now!" Kurt said. He hurried to the communication station near the far end of the room.

Bud could see Kurt's hands trembling when he picked up the phone.

"Dr. Thompson … *da*, ah, we have confirmation. There are creatures in lake …"

— 22 —

IT HAD BEEN TWO weeks since the discovery. Bud's father suggested that Bud and Sara meet him for dinner in the mess hall, as they called it around the expedition camp.

The mess hall was arranged like a typical cafeteria, with six-foot tables set up in six rows of ten. The food was prepared along one side of the room and was served around the clock to support the various work shifts of the team members. The URA team members selected their food from buffet bins behind a long, rectangular plate of glass with a food access opening above the counter where trays slid along in front of the food.

Bud and Sara sat quietly, waiting for their father, who was running late. Both watched the entrance with anticipation.

"How's your teaching going?" asked Bud.

"Okay," replied Sara. "You've been missing a lot of school lately."

"I know. Dad got me class credit for working in the expedition."

"Lucky you," Sara snapped. "But I heard Ms. Crothers complaining the other day about how much you've missed."

"Really?"

"Don't worry, I told her how busy you were making scientific discoveries." Sara rolled her eyes.

"Thanks ... I think," Bud said.

"Whatever."

"You should hang with Peter and me after class sometime," Bud offered.

"Why would I want to hang with two little—"

"Let's eat. It doesn't look like Dad is going to make it," Bud interrupted. Bud motioned for the cafeteria staff to serve them. Typically people served themselves in a buffet, but Bud's father had arranged for this meal to be a special one for them.

Just as the staff started placing the food on their table, their father arrived. "Sorry, Bud. Sorry, Sara. Just got out of our last meeting with the URA and SCAR reps."

"That's okay," Bud said.

"We have the eyes of the world on us, so these meetings have gone painfully slow. But tonight, we're celebrating. The team finally has permission to explore farther. We're going to expand the drill hole and install a transport the Germans designed for deep mine operations. It is sort of a cross between a sideways-looking subway system and a high-speed elevator."

"So you're going to install an elevator all the way down to the lake?" asked Sara.

"Basically. It will be a high-speed transport system with a clean room around the entrance."

"A transport to the lake. Awesome!" Bud said.

"What's a clean room?" asked Sara.

"A clean room makes sure people going down to the lake are free from contaminants. It is the same sort of clean room they use to make computer chips. Anyone going down to the lake will be wearing special suits that NASA designed for space exploration. That way we keep the lake from getting contaminated."

"That sounds like the clean room Larry showed me at the Space Center back home," Bud said.

Bud's father nodded. "Exactly. We'll then install the fully enclosed German transport shaft in an enlarged ice hole using the latest robotic technology from Japan."

"Are they going to install a bigger two-mile-long pipe or something?" asked Sara.

"No, we'll be creating a new, larger ice hole two hundred feet north from the present position and installing it in sections, one hundred meter section at a time. That position will take the transport down to the shore of the lake, to a landmass surrounding the lake. It will certainly be the longest elevator-type transport ever created."

"Will they have webcams down at the lake?" asked Bud.

Bud's father took a bite of food and swallowed quickly.

"Well, computer equipment and network equipment will be installed in the transport shaft, and each explorer will have a personal webcam mounted to his or her helmet to allow the worldwide Internet audience to watch every move of the explorers as they journey into the pristine lake environment."

"That's way cool," Bud said.

"So anyone with an Internet connection around the world will be able to watch?" asked Sara.

"Yep, I received approval from the White House. For the first time in history, the Internet audience is projected to be more than five hundred million people online at the same time, watching the event. All the major technology companies are joining forces to increase the bandwidth of the Internet and provide customers with the equipment needed to expand their Internet service."

Bud's father took another quick bite. He pulled out a paper while he was chewing and handed it to Sara. Bud leaned over to look.

"This is the advertisement they will be running around the world in twenty different languages," Bud's father said.

The advertisements read,

3-D computer screens in every home to explore Antarctica's under-ice world!

Journey under the ice with the science teams in real time!

A lost world is found!

"Once the expedition site transport shaft and transport are installed," Bud's father continued, "three explorers, outfitted in NASA's brand new space suits with embedded webcams, will be transported to the lake surface to begin their exploration of the lake. The event will be bigger than when Neil Armstrong took that first step on the moon."

"Nice," Bud said. "With webcams on each explorer, it'll be like we're with them as they explore the lake."

"Exactly. The worldwide audience will be watching live over the shoulder of each explorer as they journey around the mysterious lake in real time, two miles under the ice."

"Ah, great. That's just great," said Sara sarcastically as her eyes started tearing up. "Now how long will it take to get everything ready?"

Bud's father looked at Sara and continued, "It's not that bad. The Germans said they can get it installed in eight weeks with NASA working on expanding the ice hole. Intel has agreed to help install the clean room at the same time. It is pretty amazing that they can do it so quickly, but I guess they're using the equipment they built for one of the South American mines, and NASA is using some of their new space technology for the drilling. They were planning to use it on Europa."

"Eight weeks? I can't believe this. We'll be here forever," complained Sara. She threw down her fork and shoved herself back into her chair. "I want to go home! I want to go home, Dad! This place is like a prison!"

"Shhhh … lower your voice," Bud whispered. "People can hear you."

"I want to go home!" Sara said in between sobs.

"Honey," Bud's father said as he reached out to Sara. But it was too late. Sara stormed out of the cafeteria.

Bud just looked down at his food and pushed around some mashed potatoes on his plate. "Sara will be okay. She's just homesick for her friends," Bud said.

"I know. It's been hard on all of us since Mom died. I was hoping this trip would help bring us closer together," Bud's father said as he pushed his plate away from him.

"Where's Europa?" Bud asked, changing the subject as he usually did whenever talk of losing his mother came up.

"Oh, Europa is one of Jupiter's moons. They have always speculated that there were huge oceans under the ice on Europa, so NASA sent a space probe years ago that is nearing its orbit." Bud's father took another hurried bite of food from his plate that was now in the middle of the table. "I wish I could stay longer for dinner, but I have another meeting. Some general in Argentina is making threats."

"Threats? Like what?" asked Bud.

"Nothing to worry about, really. Just saying the expedition is on land owned by Argentina. It's really nothing to worry about. Oh, and I had a brief discussion with Larry. He said he was sending you a care package."

"A care package?" Bud asked.

"Yep, something about some Space Center projects you can work on while you're here," his father said. "He knows you'll be here longer now."

"That's cool. Maybe Peter can help me, too?"

"Knowing Larry, whatever he sends you will challenge you and keep you busy while they build the new transport."

Bud rolled his eyes. "Knowing Larry, I'm sure it will keep me busy."

Bud's father looked at his watch. "Can you go make sure Sara is okay?"

"Sure thing, but can I come to Mission Control with you tonight?"

"Not tonight, Bud. Maybe tomorrow. I have to go now." He stood and gave Bud a quick hug. "Love you. Please tell Sara I will talk with her tomorrow morning, okay?"

"Okay. Don't worry. She'll be fine."

Bud's father quickly left the cafeteria headed toward Mission Control.

Bud pulled out his cell phone to see if he could connect up with Peter after he checked on Sara.

— 23 —

Bud went into the family living quarters after dinner. He could hear Sara crying in her room. Bud knocked on Sara's closed door. "Sara?"

"Leave me alone!" Sara cried through the closed door.

"Dad's worried about you."

Sara didn't respond.

"I'm going to meet up with Peter at the computer room. You wanna come?"

"Why would I want to do that?" Sara said, sniffling. "Just leave me alone."

"Jeez, sorry," Bud said, looking at the closed door. "Fine, then." Bud turned away from Sara's door and went over to Casey's kennel. Casey wagged his tail frantically and barked when he saw Bud. "At least someone is happy to see me around here. Let's go, Case—Peter is waiting for us."

Bud jogged out of their living quarters toward the computer room with Casey following closely behind— slobber flying everywhere, as usual.

A short time later, in the computer room, Casey lay below the workbench, across the top of Bud's feet, chewing on a bone while Bud and Peter worked on connecting Bud's custom cell phones to the Internet.

"I think it is working now," Bud said as he checked his access to a news website. Bud noticed a video link appearing on the website with the title, "Argentina general makes threats to Antarctic expedition."

"Hey, I think this is the general my dad was telling me about at dinner tonight," Bud said. He tapped on the cell phone display, starting the video.

Peter looked over at Bud's computer screen. "General?"

"Yeah, this general thinks the expedition is on Argentina's land or something. Let's check it out."

A close-up image of General Jorge Hernandez appeared. He was pacing back and forth, his massive frame filling the video as he walked, puffing on a freshly lit cigar. The general's expression was intense; his eyes looked as if they were on fire, and the heavy lines on his face deepened as he stopped at a window and looked over a courtyard. He walked to a nearby microphone and began to speak.

"It's a sad day for the people of Argentina. That so-called Antarctic lake that has been discovered belongs to Argentina. It should be ours to control, the expedition should be mine to lead, and this infamy must not go unpunished. The world will soon know General Hernandez. The world will soon know fear—"

"Holy cow, check this dude out. This guy looks like he means business," Bud said. Peter moved his wheelchair closer to Bud.

"… You will pay. You will all pay for the injustice you have committed," the general shouted into the microphone.

The video stopped. Bud tapped his phone, activating another Internet link. A video of a news reporter began playing.

"… his heavy hand had run the country from behind the scene for years while equipping Argentina's military and training its forces. This gave him much more power than anyone else in the Argentinean government, which he appeared to enjoy, abusing it more often than not. Argentina had endured years of internal struggle and poverty. The diamond discovery Jorge's company unearthed in northeastern Paraguay promised to change all of that. Jorge used the latest technology to mine deeper and more aggressively than any other mining company in the world. His strategy paid off as he discovered new diamond fields …"

"This guy sounds scary," Peter said. "I wonder if your father knows how crazy this general really is."

The reporter in the video continued, "Jorge used his growing wealth to influence and acquire the world's most advanced military technology. Jorge felt he could push Argentina to become a world power. Most would be content to be one of the richest men in the world. But Jorge's hunger for power drove him harder and further than anyone could have imagined. With the reports of corruption and allegations of impropriety among Argentine politicians increasing, unemployment soaring, and poverty taking hold of his country, General Hernandez effectively took control of the country. The Argentine president has confirmed that he has given the general full control to make all military decisions." The video ended.

Bud selected another video of the general. The video followed the general as if he were on a reality TV show, and the footage showed him barking out commands. "Jose, Jose, prepare the men." The general continued to pace in the dark room shown in the video as he filled the room with clouds of cigar smoke. He walked slowly and confidently out of the dark room and onto a balcony overlooking a sea of cheering Argentines packed into the plaza. The video showed the large, excited crowd down below and then scanned back to the general looking out over the crowd.

"Argentina will not show weakness—"

The crowd roared, and the general continued, "We're a powerful country with strong military forces—"

The crowd roared louder. The general paused gracefully and then continued, his words gaining speed and intensity as he spoke, "The world must take notice! We have been ignored by the nations of the world far too long! We must take back our territory in Antarctica." The general's big, booming voice, radiated down over the crowd, whose cheers intensified throughout the plaza. "Now I introduce my chief of staff, Jose Perez."

The crowd roared as the general moved to allow Jose to speak. "My many thanks, my dear general. You are the greatest general in the world. You are the strongest military leader in the world!" The crowd roared louder still as Jose backed away from the microphone.

"Jeez, what a suck-up. I wonder if that guy would get shot if he disagreed with General Bully?" Bud said as he continued to watch the video.

The general's gaze intensified as the video showed a close-up of the general's face and then zoomed out to fit his entire body into the frame of the video. The general extended his chest out and shoulders back, took a big puff of his cigar, and blew it out above the crowd. The crowd roared again. He paused and then bellowed into the microphone in his deepest voice, "The world will know our power. The world will know Argentina's greatness."

The general took a deep breath and smiled, puffing harder now on the cigar. A breeze blew large clumps of cigar ashes from his half-smoked cigar over the crowd, and the ashes fell on them like snowflakes.

Bud exited the video and turned to Peter. "That guy is one crazy wackadoodle bully. I have a bad feeling about him. Why would he think we are on Argentina's land? I'm really confused."

Peter nodded. "Me, too."

— 24 —

WITH THE EXPEDITION TRANSPORT still being installed, Bud and Peter went back to focusing on their schoolwork in Ms. Crothers's classroom. After school, Bud and Peter would do more exploring around the camp ... although at times, it seemed more like spying than exploring, as Bud and Peter were able to monitor most places around the expedition camp from the comfort of the computer room.

One day, as the two boys left the classroom, Bud slowed down by Ms. Crothers's desk. She was still writing on some papers.

"Let's ask her," said Bud to Peter as they approached her desk.

"Ask me what, boys?"

"We heard there was some Argentina general saying the expedition was on land owned by Argentina," said Bud. "How can that be? We're on Antarctica, aren't we?"

"Well, we discussed geography and politics in one of the many classes you both missed," said Ms. Crothers crossly. She looked up at them over the top of her glasses.

"Oh, sorry, Ms. Crothers, we'll—" Peter started.

"Well, now, the short version is simply that a number of countries have claimed parts of Antarctica to be their land. Sort of like how Great Britain claimed land around the world years ago. You remember that from our history lesson, don't you?"

Both the boys nodded quickly.

"So the issue at hand with Argentina is that many countries don't recognize Argentina's claim to land on Antarctica."

"Countries like the US?" asked Bud.

"Exactly."

"We saw a video of a general in Argentina," Peter said. "He looks pretty mad."

"Yes, well, let's hope the international community can resolve the issues diplomatically. For now, I wouldn't be concerned."

"Thanks, Ms. Crothers," Bud said. He jumped on the back of Peter's wheelchair. "Let's go." They quickly moved out of the classroom.

Bud rode around on the back of Peter's wheelchair with its power-generating propeller. His backpack hung heavy and low on his back, causing Bud to lean forward, slightly off balance and almost on top of Peter. Casey followed close behind them, managing to catch up with the wheelchair.

Peter showed Bud how to use all the latest computer equipment in the computer room, where they quickly discovered new ways to play online games with kids around the world using their cell phones. But that eventually got boring.

Bud set up a webcast with Gregory back home using a cool two-way videophone programmed with smartphone apps that tapped into the camp's Internet backbone. But talking with Gregory quickly got boring, too. So the boys moved on to installing wireless routers acquired from one of the supply rooms all around the camp to provide them with wireless connectivity everywhere they went. They even added webcams so they could monitor what was going on around the camp—now that was fun.

Bud worked on his video helicopter. He flew it around the computer room, controlling it with his cell phone as he watched the video coming from it. "Peter, check this out." Bud showed Peter the video screen of the cell phone. It showed a video stream originating from the helicopter.

"Yeah, what about it? You showed that to me already."

"Keep watching." Bud slowly maneuvered the helicopter behind them.

"Now close your eyes and see if you can tell where it flies to next."

The helicopter made a very slight sound, almost like a slight summer breeze. Peter wrinkled his forehead in concentration.

"Now open your eyes." The helicopter was now positioned six inches from Peter's face.

"Holy cow!" Peter said in shock.

"I've added a stealth shield to buffer the noise that the helicopter motor usually makes. Cool, huh?"

"How the heck did you do that?"

"Something I learned at the Space Center. Now we can monitor places where we can't put more webcams," Bud said as he landed the helicopter on the desk in front of him and made a few adjustments.

The computer-room doors opened abruptly, causing both Bud and Peter to jump. "Is there a Bud Thompson in here?" barked a team member as he stood impatiently at the computer-room doors.

"Huh?"

"Thompson? Bud Thompson? Got a box for him," said the team member hurriedly.

"Oh, yes, that's me. I'm Bud Thompson."

"Here ya go." The team member placed the box on the table they were working at and then left.

"I know what this is." Bud smiled and started pulling at the box to get it open.

Peter just watched.

"Larry sent me a box of projects he wants me to work on for the Space Center," Bud said.

"Really? Here? He wants you to work on projects here?" Peter asked.

"Well, I suspect he just sent the stuff to me to keep me busy. I think he was thinking I was bored or something." Bud rolled his eyes.

Bud started to pull the equipment out of the box. It was arranged in plastic bags, each of which bore a label. There was a note in the box.

B-man,
Enjoy the projects. Thought you might like to add a fleet of flying robots to your helicopter.
Have fun,
Larry

"That's cool," Bud said. "Looks like we have a few more projects to work on."

— 25 —

BUD AND PETER WORKED on the kits that Larry sent, which included a half-dozen robots that resembled dragonflies but were made out of circuit boards and electrical components. The wings were made out of some sort of reinforced plastic. Bud had the first one ready to go.

"Okay, you ready for the first flight of dragonfly numero uno?"

"Sure thing, Captain." Peter smiled. He looked over to watch Bud but kept typing on his computer.

Bud tapped a few times on his cell phone. The robotic dragonfly came to life. Its wings started moving, which lifted it about one inch from the table.

Peter stopped typing to look. "Awesome!" Peter said.

"We have liftoff. Repeat, we have liftoff," Bud said, imitating Mission Control during a space flight.

Bud tapped his cell phone a few more times, causing the dragonfly to maneuver higher as it buzzed loudly and flew first to the left and then to the right. Bud started making it fly in loops.

"This is pretty cool." Bud looked over to Peter.

Just then the dragonfly made a beeline directly into the wall and hit it hard.

Wamp!

Peter started laughing.

"Looks like I have some more work to do," Bud said.

"Looks like it," Peter said as he laughed.

"You know …" started Bud.

"Uh-oh. When you say 'you know,' it's usually followed by some new feature you want to add."

"*Exactamundo.* Larry sent me a bag of minicams that can send video and audio to my cell phone. I bet he knew I would want to add them to the dragonflies. Once I assemble them, I can get all of the dragonflies to send video to my cell phone. Can you write an app for my cell phone while I work on retrofitting the dragonflies? Let's call it our video Swarm."

"Already on it," Peter said as his typing intensified.

After about an hour, Bud had all of the dragonflies working.

"Here," Peter directed, "download the app called Swarm. It will allow you to control all the dragonflies simultaneously and watch video from them, too."

"Okay, here goes nothing." Bud tapped furiously on his cell phone. All the dragonflies were flapping their wings and buzzing loudly.

"Cool. Looks like they're working."

Bud smiled. "Yep."

Peter stopped what he was typing and looked at the hovering dragonflies flying in formation. "Those are amazing," Peter said as he leaned over to get a view of Bud's cell-phone screen. Six videos were coming in from the dragonflies, each of which was hovering an inch from the table.

A few more taps, and Bud had them flying around near the ceiling. A few more taps, and he positioned them at each corner of the room, with two hovering two inches from the middle of the ceiling.

"Cool. The video is awesome!"

"Yep," Bud agreed. "Now we can get video and audio anywhere in the camp … although the battery is only good for thirty minutes, and I need to add my stealth feature, so they're not so noisy."

"Isn't this sort of like spying on people?" asked Peter.

"Nah, think of it as our own version of reality TV. Besides, nothing going on in the camp is supposed to be private, right? At least that's what Kurt said. So think of it as our video log of the expedition." Bud grinned.

"I guess you're right," Peter said reluctantly.

"Besides, it will keep us informed on what is going on, so we can help out," Bud said. He gathered the dragonflies and a variety of tools and contraptions the boys had built and placed them in his backpack, along with portable chargers for their cell phones. Bud added a variety of other electronic devices.

"Won't they see them flying above their heads?" asked Peter.

"Maybe, but the ceilings are so high, I don't think most people will notice them," Bud said.

Peter shook his head and went back to typing.

$$-26-$$

Bud wore his heavy backpack everywhere; it had become Bud and Peter's portable lab kit. The boys found entertainment in adding additional "features," as they called them, all over the expedition camp. Bud used his dragonflies for recon to make sure the coast was clear to add "features," which included wireless webcams at strategic locations Peter mapped out around the facility. The boys could access the cameras using their cell phones to monitor what was going on around them. They even installed audio-monitoring equipment and motion detectors.

Bud and Peter were most curious about what was going on in the places they were told they weren't allowed to enter, like the Mission Control room when Bud's father wasn't with them. Since all the action took place in Mission Control, it seemed the only way to know what was going on was to add "features" to the room.

"C'mon," Peter said as he grabbed Bud's arm. "Let's go to Mission Control."

"We can't. My dad isn't in there now. What are you doing?"

"I got us access. We can install a wireless webcam in there."

"Are you crazy?"

"Nope. I sent the security guard on duty an e-mail telling him we had some maintenance to perform in the room."

"Right, sure, you sent an e-mail. After all, he will take orders from the two of us old guys. Jeez, have you lost it?" Bud was walking at a furious pace as he tried to keep up with Peter's wheelchair, occasionally bumping into someone walking down the hallway.

"Whoops, sorry," one of the team members said on her way by. "Slow down. What's the rush?"

Bud looked back and didn't see Casey anywhere. Bud knew that Casey could eventually find his way back to their living quarters, so he didn't worry.

"We have ten minutes to install the webcam and wireless router. The majority of the team is currently at an all-hands meeting in the pressroom. Now's the time, Bud."

"Sure, I get it. Gee, Mr. Security Guard, just let us install our webcam, so we can keep tabs on what is happening in the *restricted* Mission Control room," Bud said in a huff, shaking his head. "What the heck—we should see if the security guard could help us install them, too!"

"Bud, please. Work with me here. Just keep your trap shut and follow my lead."

"But someone is going to notice the webcams we've installed, won't they?" asked Bud.

"There's so much electronic equipment all around the camp, there's no way anyone will figure out that our webcams aren't supposed to be there," Peter said with confidence.

Bud rolled his eyes as he tried to catch his breath. Just ahead were the double doors marked "Mission Personnel Only—Controlled Access." Bud's heart began to race.

Peter slowed down enough to gracefully pass through the double doors with Bud hanging on behind. The doors swung closed with a thud as they briefly caught on Bud's backpack, nearly throwing Bud off balance.

"May I help you two?" asked the large, muscular security guard in a deep, low voice that would cause anyone to stand up straight and listen.

Peter came to an abrupt stop and looked up.

"Yes, sir. Are you Ben Garty?"

"Yes, young man, I am Mr. Garty," the security guard said as his muscles appeared to flex, causing his oversized chest to puff up like a blowfish.

"You should have received an e-mail regarding a work order, Mr. Garty—from Dr. Popov?" Peter said confidently.

The security guard instantly stopped powering up his muscles. The air appeared to abruptly exit, leaving his muscles in a deflated state. The security guard's voice softened and was higher pitched.

"Ah, yes, sir, sorry. I wasn't expecting—" the security guard started to say as his face grew red. "… yes, well, Dr. Popov sent me an e-mail just before my shift telling me to expect two technicians. I just wasn't expecting two—"

Peter interrupted. "No problem at all, Mr. Garty. We get that all the time. It should only take us a couple of minutes. You know how it is; we're helping around camp while the other team members are tied up in meetings."

The embarrassed security guard quickly left the room to the two boys to perform their maintenance. He went into one of the offices on the far side of the room and closed the door.

"Well, that's a first! I guess we're now the youngest technicians on the base, too," Bud said as he shook his head in amazement.

"Yes, something like that … as per Dr. Popov," Peter said with a devious smile.

Bud started making fun of Peter's conversation. "Yes, sir, Mr. Farty, we're here to watch over you, Mr. Smarty-pants."

"Bud, please! Let's hurry!" Peter showed Bud where to install the two wireless webcams and an Internet router in the corners above the room. "Position them in that location and that location," directed Peter.

"But won't they see them?" asked Bud as he strained to put in the last screw.

"Nope. Look at all the equipment in this place. No one will notice. Trust me. Everyone will assume the additional equipment is supposed to be there."

Just as they were finishing up, a thump and then a couple of loud scratches came from the two double doors leading into the hallway. Both Bud's and Peter's heads turned at the same time in panic as they realized Casey was trying to join them.

Bud quickly completed the connection of an antenna and then jumped on the back of Peter's wheelchair and headed for the door. He reached the door just in time as the security guard walked out of the office wondering what the scratching was all about.

"Thank you, Ben. Our work here is done," Peter said and then quickly maneuvered through the double doors with Bud hanging on the back of the wheelchair. Casey barked and ran after the boys as Peter picked up speed down the hallway.

Bud looked back in time to see the security guard push through the double doors, giving them one last look as he shook his head.

Bud smiled as they turned the corner away from the Mission Control room and out of sight.

Casey barked when he finally caught up with Peter and Bud, slobber flying in big globs everywhere. One glob landed on Bud's leg.

Bud jumped off the wheelchair. "Aw, that's gross, Case," Bud said as he wiped his leg off and started walking with Casey.

— 27 —

BUD AND PETER WERE back in the computer room, typing away on their computers, when Sara walked in.

"Hey, Sara," Bud said.

"Don't get too excited. I don't plan on staying long," said Sara.

She sat down, fidgeting in the chair next to them, looking around the room.

"You look bored," Bud said as he glanced at Sara.

"No kidding. Really? Why would I be bored, anyway? This expedition has gone on forever. After all, there is plenty to do in this prison of a place," Sara said, firing off her words as rapidly as a machine gun. She continued in a sarcastic tone, "Not!"

"Jeez, all right, already. Sorry I said anything. Here, use this—I have it set up now to connect to your friends back home." Bud handed the cell phone to Sara and continued, "But it only has the external speaker working at the moment."

"For real?" Sara looked at the phone and tapped the screen; it made dialing sounds and then connected. Sara's face lit up as soon as she heard the voice of her friend.

"Hello?"

"Hi, Lisa!"

Bud imitated the way Sara was talking to her friend. Sara hit him and focused again on the cell-phone screen.

"Sara! How are you?" asked Lisa. "We thought you were supposed to be home already."

"Yeah, me too. It's a long story. So tell me, what's news? Like tell me all the latest gossip," Sara said eagerly.

"We just returned from Key West. The entire gang went for graduation. Oh, my God, it was like so totally cool. Jamie hooked up with that cute nerd Little Sammy."

Bud looked at Sara. "Way to go, Little Sammy!"

Sara elbowed him as Lisa continued, "And—"

The screen went black, and the cell phone beeped. The connection was lost. "Hey! What did you do?" complained Sara.

"Peter, what happened?" asked Bud.

"Sorry about that. I'm still working on the network. I think there is a massive amount of data being transferred from the camp right now that kicks us off the Internet. But I'll get that fixed," Peter said as he typed faster on his keyboard.

Sara put her face in her hands, obviously trying not to cry in front of them. Sara mumbled from behind her hands, "My friends are having a great time without me. This stupid trip is never going to end."

"I still need to update the Berkeley lab team using our dedicated connection," Peter said as he looked at Sara. "You want to meet my friend Tom Sutton? He's a computer engineering graduate student who started college about the time most kids start high school. He also works for my father."

Sara gave Peter a curious look. "Why would I want to talk to one of your nerdy friends?"

"Fine, forget it," Peter snapped back.

"C'mon, just talk with him," Bud said. "After all, he's at the same school you want to go to next year."

Sara stared at Bud for a moment. "I guess. At least I'll be talking to someone away from this place."

Peter established the connection using the cell phone with video enabled, and Tom's face showed up on the cell-phone screen.

"Hi, Tom!" Peter said.

"Peter, what's going on? We're kind of busy here, but it's always great to see you. Is everything okay? Did you want to talk with your father?"

"I don't need to talk with him. Everything's looking good our end. I just wanted to give you an update that we're on schedule."

"Excellent," Tom said.

Sara looked over Peter's shoulder at the cell-phone screen and did a double take when she saw Tom. She blushed and elbowed Peter.

"Introduce me," Sara whispered.

"Oh, ah, Tom, this is my friend Sara. She's Dr. Thompson's daughter."

Peter handed the phone to Sara. She held it up to her face. "Hi, Tom. I'm Sara."

"Ah, hi, ah, Sara. I'm Tom. Oh, but Peter already told you that, so I ..."

Peter moved his wheelchair to another computer, with Bud and Casey following behind him. Bud sat down at the computer next to Peter and started surfing the web. As much as the boys tried not to listen, they could still hear Sara's conversation over the cell phone's speaker.

"It's nice talking to someone away from this place," Sara said. "I'm trying to get into UC Berkeley once the expedition is over. So you're in charge of all the Berkeley computer equipment?" Sara was talking faster now.

Bud leaned over to Peter and whispered, "I think she likes Tom. She always talks fast when she likes a boy." They both snickered and then stopped abruptly when Sara shot them both a look. Bud turned away and locked his eyes on the computer screen directly in front of him.

Peter just shook his head, grinning.

"Well, umm, not really," Tom said. "But I do get to assist Dr. Roberts, who is the engineering department chair."

"Dr. Roberts?"

"Yeah, you know—Peter's father,"

"Oh, yeah, Bud told me that. Hey, what's it like to go to college at seventeen?" asked Sara.

"Well, I actually received my computer science degree at seventeen, and I'm working on my master's degree now. I actually started at fourteen ..."

Bud was finally able to focus on the computer in front of him and shut out Sara's conversation.

It wasn't long after the initial introduction to Tom when Bud realized Sara was following Peter and Bud around to get opportunities to call Tom on the video cell phone that Bud continued to work on. Bud set up another cell phone so he could give one to Sara.

Sara and Tom talked on the cell phone often while Bud and Peter worked on their projects in the computer lab.

"I think Sara is falling for him," whispered Bud.

"Ditto. I think Tom likes Sara a lot, too," Peter said.

Peter pointed to Sara, who was staring intently at Tom on the cell-phone screen. "Looks like they're becoming a pretty hot item," Peter said.

Bud shook his head. "Well, at least she stopped complaining so much."

Sara got up from the chair she was sitting on. "I'm going back to the school. I have another class to teach," Sara said as she floated out of the room.

Bud waved to Sara without looking at her as she left abruptly. Bud and Peter looked at each other.

"Amazing. She has actually stopped complaining entirely!" said Bud.

They both snickered.

Bud scanned the research-center webcams. He connected to the channel 17 webcam at the UC Berkeley lab when he noticed they seemed to be excited about something.

"Hey, Peter, check this out," Bud said. "It looks like something is happening at your father's lab."

Bud turned up the volume, so they could hear audio and watch video on their computer.

"Tom?" said Peter's father.

"Ah, yes, Dr. Roberts?" asked Tom, trying not to appear startled.

"Tom, how would you like to join the URA expedition for a few weeks?" asked Dr. Roberts.

Bud's eyes got big as he watched the video.

"What? Really? Wow! I would love to go!"

Bud and Peter grinned at each other.

"Well, then, you better get out of here and get your bags packed. You're leaving on a chartered plane in two hours. They need a computer expert at the expedition pronto, and you're that guy," said Dr. Roberts as he left the room.

"Cool! Whoa! Wow! This is going to be so cool!" Tom danced around the computer room with a mile-wide grin. "Now I get to meet Sara in person! Boy, is she going to be surprised!"

Tom called his computer administrator backup to take over for him. "Awesome!" Tom said as he left the computer lab to prepare for his flight to the expedition camp.

Peter and Bud disconnected the link to the Berkeley computer room.

"We should tell Sara," Peter said.

"Nah, let's surprise her." Bud tapped on his cell phone. "I'm almost finished connecting the monitoring devices we installed to our cell phones. I have a few more adjustments to make to my heli and the Swarm."

They continued working on their monitoring project, which allowed them to tune in to activity going on all over camp. Their system was working nicely.

Sara returned to the videophone later that evening with Casey. Casey jumped up on Peter and then ran to Bud and barked.

"Bud, when are you coming back to our quarters? Casey is missing you," Sara said. Without waiting for a response, she continued, "Peter, can you show me how to connect back to Tom?"

Bud rolled his eyes, knowing she just wanted to talk with Tom again.

"Sorry. You won't be able to talk with Tom tonight," Peter said.

"Huh? Why not? Are there problems?"

"It's technical," Bud said as he winked at Peter.

"Okay, I'll just try again tomorrow."

Bud and Peter looked at each other, trying not to laugh.

Sara grabbed one of the cell phones Bud had been working on from the desk. It had wires and other attachments hanging out of it that were not normally part of a cell phone.

"Hmm, maybe I can use this to call him tomorrow. Does this thing work now?" asked Sara.

"Yep," Peter said. "The internet connection works, so you should be able to call from your room."

"Cool!" Sara said. She left the room, skipping and humming a song.

Bud and Peter looked at each other again and started laughing.

"I better go," Bud said as he gave Peter a fist bump. "See ya tomorrow at school."

— 28 —

BUD'S FATHER HAD ARRANGED for the family to have a private dinner together, since the last one had not gone very well—although this one wasn't starting out any better.

"They're not serving us tonight?" asked Bud, who was watching for their father to arrive.

"Not tonight," Sara said. "No clue when Dad will arrive, so he said just to start without him."

They moved their trays along the buffet and made their selections.

"Sure miss Grams's cookin'," Bud said, trying to make small talk with Sara.

Sara ignored him as they made their way back to a private table along the far back wall of the cafeteria.

Sara dropped her tray with a thump on the table. "This food is disgusting," she snapped.

"Aw, jeez, here we go—" started Bud until he saw his father entering the cafeteria. "Here comes Dad. He's fixing his plate."

"Finally," Sara grumbled.

"Hi, kids!" Bud's father said as he sat down at the table.

"How's the lake transport install coming along, Dad?" asked Bud.

"Oh, it's coming along," Bud's father said, looking off into the distance as he quickly tried to swallow an oversized bite of mashed potatoes. "It should be ready in a few more days. We have people working around the clock and have flown in equipment from all over the world. It's amazing how so many people from around the world have worked together to expedite the installation. I don't think anyone thought it could be possible to complete such a major project in only eight weeks."

"You going down to the lake, too?" Bud asked.

"No, no. We have three astronauts going down there. We're using the latest space suits from NASA to make sure we don't contaminate the lake environment."

"I keep hearing that the probe data shows there is bioluminescence-generated light all around the lake. What the heck does bioluminescence mean?" asked Bud.

"That's a really good question. Yes, the scientists currently believe that a great deal of the production and emission of light is coming from biological sources, but light also appears to be generated by mineral sources surrounding the lake, too."

"Biological? You mean, plants are generating light? How can that happen?"

"Well, life has a way of evolving uniquely based upon its environment. With no sunlight down there, it seems that nature has managed to evolve to provide its own light." Bud's father looked at Sara. "How you doing, sweetie?"

Sara took a long breath. "Well, I've been trying to keep busy by teaching and working on my lesson plan for the kids. But I really miss my friends."

"I'm sure your friends don't miss you!" joked Bud.

"Bud, please. That was uncalled for," Bud's father said sternly.

"Tell Dad about the boy you like," Bud said.

"Shut up, you—" Sara said as she started to blush.

"Now, kids, please. I know it's hard on all of us here, but I want to try to have at least one nice meal together, all right?" Bud's father said. "Just think, we're making history here in Antarctica. We've discovered an underground world that has evolved for thousands, if not millions, of years, with its own ecosystem. And we now know there are new species of fish we have never seen before. Who knows what life has evolved down there?"

Sara rolled her eyes.

Bud got serious. "I think there are dinos down there. I know I saw something. Are they exploring at all? Have they found anything?"

"Well, son, we'll find out soon enough. Unfortunately, they put off exploring to focus on building the transport." He quickly changed the subject. "So how's Peter doing?"

"He's doing good. He knows a lot about computers, and we've explored the camp together," Bud said as he thought about all the "features" they had added to the camp with a little bit of guilt.

"I know his father pretty well. He's the computer-engineering department chair at UC Berkeley, where Sara wants to go."

Sara looked up at the mention of UC Berkeley.

Bud smiled and said, "Sara knows one of his students." Bud started laughing, waving his index finger back and forth at Sara.

"Bud!" snapped Sara.

"One of his students? Who's that?"

"A boy named Tom Sutton. He's really nice," Sara said. She started to fidget.

"I know of Tom. He's one of Dr. Roberts's young protégés. In fact —"

Bud interrupted him before he could mention that Tom was coming to the expedition camp. "So how you doing, Dad?" asked Bud.

His father gave him a quizzical look. "Oh, I'm fine. There's just a great deal of stress trying to keep the expedition moving. I know we've been here a while now, and it sure would be good to get you both back home." Bud's father looked directly at Sara.

Sara shook her head as tears filled her eyes.

Bud changed the subject again, so he didn't have to hear Sara complain. "Are you excited about what you might find down at the lake?"

"Sure. The expedition is exciting. But all the politics are challenging. To top it off, we just found out the Argentineans are whining again about their quote, unquote territory." Bud's father took another bite of his meal.

"I know. Peter and I were looking at some videos. That Argentine general is really crazy. Is there any kind of real threat from that bully?"

"No. I've been told we have insiders who say he is just making idle threats and rattling his saber. I don't think there is anything to worry about." His father took another bite of food and swallowed quickly. "Well, I better get back to Mission Control. We're working toward the first mission to the lake in a few days. We have a great deal of work to do." He gave Bud and Sara a hug. "Love you guys," he said quickly as he hurried off to work.

"I heard Tom likes you," Bud said.

Sara just looked at Bud with a blank stare.

"Yep ... I heard he would really like to meet you."

"Really?" Sara's entire demeanor changed.

"Well, gotta go. Peter has me helping him with some system testing."

"Wait, Bud. He likes me?"

"Yep, I heard he really likes you," Bud said again. "Gotta go meet Peter. See ya later." Bud dashed out of the cafeteria.

— 29 —

Bud tightened the last screw on the helicopter. He engaged the motor, and the blades whirled around so fast that Bud couldn't see them. Even more amazingly, the blades didn't blow around any air.

"How'd you do that, Bud?" Peter said.

"I call it my superstealth heli. Pretty cool, huh? I just upgrade the noise suppressor to counter the airflow and violà—no more bursts of air. I'm going to upgrade the dragonflies with the same suppressors, too. But that will take more time."

Peter nodded with approval. "Nice job. That's impressive. So you can control the heli with your cell phone anywhere in camp and watch the video?"

"Yep, it will fly anywhere around camp now that we added the wireless routers. I'm going to fly it down the hallway to see how it works. I'll use the phone display to guide it as I watch the video." Bud tapped on his cell phone, and the video started. Peter moved closer to Bud, so he could watch the video.

The helicopter flew out of the computer room and into the hallway, hovering one foot from the ceiling.

Bud and Peter watched the video as they went down one hallway and then another. Team members walking down the hallway didn't notice the silent helicopter flying five feet over their heads.

"This is really cool," Peter said. "No one notices the heli, and this video is nice and sharp—it doesn't bounce around. Can you adjust the sound, so we can hear people below?"

Bud tapped the cell phone screen a few times. "Yep, I was just adjusting the audio to it. It has a directional microphone on it, so it only listens to where it is pointed."

"Try it on those two people coming down that hallway," Peter said as he pointed to the video on the cell-phone screen.

Bud tapped his phone and placed the heli above the two people walking in the hallway. The tiny aircraft followed the two people. "Let me point it ... okay, now let me turn it up and put it on speaker," Bud said.

Suddenly audio was coming from the cell phone. The heli had matched the walkers' speed and was following them in autopilot mode with its audio microphone pointed down at them from above.

"My eyes are killing me," the team member said. "These hours are crazy."

"I know what you mean; it seems like we're always working. At least the shifts may get back to normal once the transport is operational ..."

Bud turned the volume down.

"It works!" Peter gave Bud a fist bump.

"Nice job. Now all we need to do is add this to the Swarm app, and the heli can fly with the dragonflies."

Bud flew the helicopter around camp, down a hallway, into offices with their doors open, and into the cafeteria. Everyone appeared very busy. No one noticed the helicopter flying silently near the ceiling above. He maneuvered the helicopter down the hallway and made it hover there as he watched the video.

"Hey, isn't that Kurt on the cell phone?" Bud asked.

"Yep. You want to listen—" started Peter.

"Exactly what I was thinking," interrupted Bud. "He told me and my dad when we first arrived that there weren't any secrets around the expedition, so why not?"

Peter smirked. "I'm sure a couple of secrets would never stop you anyway."

Bud positioned the helicopter directly above Kurt, who was pacing back and forth in the hallway. He moved the directional microphone to point at the Russian scientist and matched the movement of the helicopter with Kurt's pacing.

"*Da*," Kurt said. "*Da. Da*. Transport is nearly complete." Kurt paused and stopped pacing.

Bud adjusted the controls for the helicopter to hover over his head. "He sure sounds serious."

"Boy, does he ever," Peter said.

"General?" Kurt paused, and his voice became shaky. "I just learned there are diamonds. Transport install team detected large diamonds. Many diamonds. This has not been made public."

Laughter—loud laughter—could be heard coming from Kurt's phone. Kurt tapped on his cell phone and placed it back in his pocket.

Bud and Peter looked at each other with stunned looks.

"General? Did you hear him say general?" Peter asked.

"Yep. I wonder … nah, but diamonds?" Bud said. "Holy cow. They found diamonds down at the lake? Let's get over there quick. I need to tell my dad what Kurt said."

Peter took off in his wheelchair toward Mission Control, with Bud hanging on the back and Casey panting close behind. They were well on their way when they saw Sara.

"Slow down. There's Sara."

Peter slowed down and stopped in front of Sara.

"Guess who I heard just arrived at camp?" Bud said quickly to Sara.

"Who?"

"That boy you like … the one named Tom," Bud said, looking back at Casey, who was struggling to catch up.

"What? Are you kidding? When?" Sara asked.

"I heard they needed a computer expert and asked for him," Peter said. Casey finally caught up and barked at them, his saliva flying everywhere as he attempted to jump up onto Peter's lap in his wheelchair. "Casey, get down." Peter gave Casey a nudge away from his wheelchair.

"Where is Tom staying? Do you know?" Sara asked.

"I hear he's working in the computer center by mission control right now," Peter said as he started moving his wheelchair slowly down the hallway.

"C'mon, we need to go," Bud said. "Something else just happened I need to tell Dad about. Let's get moving. You coming, Sara?"

"What just happened?" Sara asked.

"Not sure, exactly. But we heard Kurt talking—" Bud stopped in midsentence.

"About what?" Sara asked.

"Ah, just come on—let's go," Bud said, avoiding the question so he wouldn't have to explain how he had eavesdropped on Kurt. He had just realized he would need to figure out how to explain that to his father, too.

Bud jumped on the back of Peter's already moving wheelchair, and the three of them quickly moved down the hallway in the direction of Mission Control with Casey barely keeping up behind them.

A few minutes later, they passed the computer room.

"Wait a second," Sara said as she opened the computer room doors and saw Tom typing on the computer.

"Hurry!" Bud said to Sara as Peter stopped the wheelchair. Bud took out his cell phone and started watching the video from the Mission Control room. Team members were moving around frantically.

"Hey, you!" Sara said to Tom.

"Hi, Sara!" Tom stood up and gave her a quick hug.

"Great to finally meet in person," Sara said.

Tom looked back at his computer. "Kind of busy right now. They have me working on a couple of hot problems. Can I meet you later, Sara?" He sat down while looking back at Sara.

"Sure. I'll be at the school. Come over when you can. I'll be in room Delta-Two," Sara said in the sweetest voice Bud had ever heard.

Peter and Bud watched impatiently. "Sara, c'mon! We gotta go," Bud said.

"See you later, Tom," Sara said happily.

"Aw, jeez," Bud said as he jumped back on Peter's wheelchair.

"C'mon, let's go!" Peter said eagerly.

Sara smiled smugly at Bud and Peter and then started walking in the direction of the school.

"Guess she's not coming with us," Peter said.

"She's obviously distracted. Step on it," Bud said as Casey barked.

— 30 —

THE MISSION CONTROL ROOM was busy when they arrived. Bud's father was too busy to interrupt, so Bud and Peter sat down at Peter's computer station.

Bud watched Kurt with curiosity.

"We're almost ready to go, comrade," Kurt said. His voice was amplified over the intercom in the large, crowded room. The room had been configured with pickup microphones, so everyone could hear what was going on.

Kurt continued, "The transport shaft has been secured using robotic technology, and equipment has been installed. We now complete world's largest elevator transport. It's nearly 3.6 kilometers, or 2.24 miles. Latest readings indicate a distance of 4,079 feet, or approximately 1,243 meters, from lake surface to inside of ice dome at highest point. Additional scanning probes found surrounding mountains to be 3.2 kilometers, or approximately two miles, from lake shoreline. This region filled with large amount of plant life."

Kurt's assistant added, "We have not confirmed the light source. Dr. Thompson, our best guess is that your earlier hypothesis is quite possibly correct. Light appears to originate within the environment from the mountain cliffs surrounding the region due to a mineral-chemical-electrical reaction, possibly the result of some yet unknown microbe. The light generated radiates off of the ice dome, reflecting light across the entire lake region—"

Kurt interrupted, "Also discovered that there are light-dark cycles. Light appears to slowly increase to maximum brightness then slowly decrease to minimum light levels, further suggesting biological source may be facilitating light-cycle process."

"Any idea on the biological source?" asked Bud's father.

"Yes, comrade," replied Kurt. "Biological source may occur on surrounding mountains from possible microbe generating electrical current that is reacting with crystals in mountains."

"What about the wind? Where is it coming from?" asked Bud's father.

"We're still not clear how that is happening, Dr. Thompson," answered Kurt's assistant. "There may be many volcanic tubes surrounding the lake, allowing air circulation within the environment."

"Did you find any mammalian or reptilian life?"

"Only fish found earlier, comrade; however, we're not able to explore beyond a small area around the transport at the moment. Video has confirmed environment does contain grasses, plants, and trees. Also recently installed twenty-five motion sensors with our remote-controlled vehicle recently to detect motion. We will know if anything moves in the area around the sensors."

Bud's eyes grew large as he listened. He configured his computer to display the motion-detector data readout on his screen.

"Incredible," said Bud's father. "Are the explorers ready?"

"Yes, sir," Kurt's assistant said. "They're outfitted in NASA space suits and ready to go."

"Okay, then, send them in tomorrow morning during the peak of the light cycle," ordered Bud's father.

Bud looked around the control room at the large, colorful, three-dimensional computer displays of the environment. He looked at his computer screen, which showed that motion had been detected. Bud waved to his father as he pointed to the motion-detector readings. The readings were glowing red, indicating the sensors had detected movement and recorded sounds.

Bud's father headed over to Bud while checking with the team members throughout the room as he walked.

Bud's eyes got big. "I told you. There are creatures down there!" Bud said as his father came close to where he was sitting.

Bud's father just nodded without really listening to what Bud said as he looked at the monitors around the Mission Control room. He moved close to Bud and whispered, "I saw the sensor readings, too, but right now, we don't know for sure. There could be any number of reasons why the motion detectors are detecting movement."

"We also heard Kurt—" started Bud.

His father snapped back nervously, "Please keep your voice down, Bud."

"Sorry. I just got excited." Bud sank down in his seat.

"Heard Kurt? What did you hear?" asked his father, who was only inches away from Bud's face.

Bud realized now wasn't the time to bring up how he had overheard Kurt's conversation or that he had heard him mention a general on his cell phone. He let out a breath and replied, "It's not important."

Peter looked over at Bud as his father moved on to check in with other team members.

"Don't worry about it," Peter said while typing on his wheelchair. "Your father is just busy right now. We can tell him later."

"Yeah, I guess," Bud said, feeling somewhat deflated. "I think I'll head back to school now and take that math exam Ms. Crothers has been nagging us about before tomorrow's exploration activities. I think the deadline is tomorrow, anyway. Do you need my help still?"

"No, go ahead. I have a few more hours of diagnostic tests I need to run before tomorrow that I can handle by myself. But Ms. Crothers told me I have to take the final before tomorrow's noon deadline. Will you cover for me here in the morning so I can take it? Everything will be set up and ready to go for tomorrow before I leave tonight."

"Sure thing, *no problemo*," Bud agreed. "Pretty crazy that they have school test deadlines for us with everything we're doing to help with the expedition. See ya later tomorrow morning." Bud threw his backpack over his shoulder and headed out the door.

— 31 —

THE NEXT MORNING, MISSION Control was busy. The entire team had arrived early to prepare for the first manned exploration of the lake area. Unfortunately for Peter, he was still in Ms. Crothers's classroom, taking his exam.

Bud sat down at the computer near where Peter normally sat and started looking at the sensor data, which showed more motion. Peter had left Bud a list of notes with sensors to check while Peter was taking his exam. If anything urgent came up, Bud told Peter, Bud would immediately request that Peter be released from class to come to mission control. They would deal with Ms. Crothers later.

Bud looked up at the clock display. It read "0830."

"It is time," Bud's father said over the intercom.

Bud didn't think twice as he followed his father and Kurt to the clean-room entrance adjacent to the Mission Control room. Bud looked suspiciously at Kurt, but this was still not the time or place to talk with his father about what he heard from his helicopter. Besides, Bud was still trying to figure out how to tell his father why he was flying around a helicopter listening to people's conversations. He needed to figure out how to tell him without sounding creepy, but he was starting to realize that the superstealth heli really was creepy.

Bud watched the three explorers through the thick glass wall as they neared the clean-room entrance. They moved slowly, with full space suits and helmets on, wearing heavy oxygen tanks on their backs. Each explorer had a flag on his or her helmet representing each major participant: one from the United States, one from Russia, and two flags for the combined Australia and New Zealand team.

Bud's father nodded at each explorer as each one walked into the clean room. Bud stood by his father's side and imitated him, trying to synchronize his nod with his father's nod.

Kurt looked oddly at Bud, but Bud just ignored him.

Bud's father turned to Kurt. "Is each explorer's webcam online?"

"Da."

"Then let's do this. Good luck, ladies and gentlemen," Bud's father said into a microphone that was broadcast over the intercom and into the explorers' helmet speakers.

Bud's cell phone beeped. It was a text message from Peter.

"Bud, please," said his father in an embarrassed tone.

"Sorry, Dad. Peter just finished his exam and wants me to help him carry back printouts of the probe test results. Can I go help him?"

"Sure, sure. Now let's see, where was I? Please excuse the interruption, Kurt," Bud's father said.

Once Bud had sent a text message to Peter that his father had given the okay, he quickly left Mission Control and walked toward the school section of the expedition camp to meet Peter. Bud connected his cell phone to the webcam the boys had placed in the Mission Control room and watched it as he walked.

"Hey, I should get the other phone with my logging video app to record all the action," mumbled Bud. "I'll just stop by the room and pick it up real quick."

As he walked, Bud watched the video playing on his cell phone, which came from the transport webcam. One of the explorers pressed the large, brightly lit button with her thick glove, causing the tram-transport doors to close and engage the elevator transport. The transport roared as it began the high-speed descent to lake level.

Bud touched his cell phone to switch webcams back to the control room. He saw his father and Kurt moving to their assigned positions in the control room.

"They just reached the surface, sir," Kurt said. "The team members began calling out the status of the telemetry. Temperature: 78 degrees Fahrenheit; oxygen: breathable; lighting: moderate blue and red wavelengths; water temperature: 68 degrees; wind: slight breeze of 1 mile per hour."

The control room fell silent as everyone studied the incoming data.

"Kurt, where is my video and audio feed? I want to talk with each explorer as they look around down there."

"We're working on it, sir." Kurt turned to the computer control engineer, who was typing frantically.

"Where the hell is that kid who flew in—Tom?" Bud's father said nervously.

"He's in the computer room working on it, sir," said the engineer. "Tom just got in a few nights ago and has been working on it since his arrival."

Bud could see Tom in one of the video boxes on the main display screen. Tom's fingers were flying over the computer keyboard. It reminded Bud of how Peter typed.

"Tom needed to rewrite all code after finding it was written to work with small probe cameras and not the full video camera the NASA space suits are outfitted with," reported Kurt.

"Jeez, how could they leave this for the last minute?" Bud mumbled. *I bet Tom is totally stressed*, Bud thought as he watched the video on his cell phone, almost bumping into a team member as he slowly walked down the hallway.

Tom pressed the intercom. "Sir, the system should be ready now. Go ahead and try it."

"Here we go, comrades." Kurt pressed the power button on the control panel. The display came to life, flickering and flashing on the main control-room screen. The picture was blurred.

"Can you focus the picture, Tom?" asked Bud's father.

Tom was still adjusting the controls. "Got it. Try it now," Tom said.

Bud switched to another webcam in the Mission Control room that allowed him to see the big screen better.

Finally, the video came to life, depicting three URA scientists discussing the scene, joining the conversation in midsentence. Bud stopped in the middle of the hallway. He was captivated.

"… believe it. It is amazing down here. It is almost like a jungle in the Amazon. But everything has a light purple hue to it. It's hard to explain. There are also sparkling white shining moths and the most incredibly colored glowing butterflies, along with other illuminated flying insects that seem to be floating through the air and chasing each other around. Everything is alive down here. Some leaves are dark, and others appear to glow white. Are you getting any of this, Mission Control?" asked the American team member.

"We're receiving the telemetry and have begun retransmission to the world over the Internet. You all are making history. Yet another small step for us and a large step for—" Bud's father said before being interrupted by the Russian explorer.

"Yes, yes. We are aware. Can we begin exploring lakeshore? We are eager, comrade," the Russian explorer said.

"Sure, move out as we discussed during the briefing," Bud's father said over his video communication link. "That way, you'll cover as much ground as possible. But be careful. We don't know what kind of animal life has evolved in this environment."

Bud tapped his phone screen and then looked closer at his display, which was now split into three explorer sections. He turned the noise filters on to cancel out the Mission Control background noise, allowing him to hear the explorers talk more clearly. Each section displayed the video feed from one of the explorers at lake level. The American began walking directly inland, while the Australian took a tangential course away from the lake.

The Russian struck out across the lakeshore, inspecting the plants. Both the American and Australian explorers maneuvered slowly in the mud around the large-leaved plants and through the shallow water and tall grasses as they continued to move away from the lake. Colorful, glowing insects, some large and others much smaller, floated in the air everywhere they looked.

The Russian crouched down and inspected the mud near the lake's edge. Tiny, sparkling rocks were scattered all around the area. The Russian was one hundred feet from the transport along the shore.

"Dr. Thompson?" asked the Russian.

"Yes, this is Dr. Thompson—go ahead."

"Comrade, I have confirmed the earlier probe readings. There are hundreds of diamonds scattered all around the area. They're quite large—what is this? There also appears to be large, ah, footprints in mud here," said the Russian explorer nervously, while pointing his webcam around the area and then down at the footprints for the Mission Control room to see. The footprints appeared to be the size of an elephant's and were sunk deep down in the mud due to the weight of the creature.

"I knew it," Bud said as he continued to watch in the middle of the hallway, slowly inching his way toward his living quarters to retrieve his recording cell phone before picking up Peter at the school.

The command center could see the shiny diamonds shimmering in the white-purple light spread around the shoreline. A technician monitoring the transmission in the command center said, "Sir, there are hundreds of very large diamonds scattered all over the area, and those footprints—"

A small splash, then another splash, and a swirling noise could be heard off in the distance. The Russian looked up. "Did you hear that, mission control?" asked the Russian.

Bud's father looked around the noisy control room, and everyone was shaking their heads. "No one heard anything here."

But Bud had heard the splash, since his cell phone had filtered out the control-room background noise.

"I knew it. I just knew it," Bud said, turning up the volume.

Another splash—this time closer. The Russian explorer looked over the lake with his webcam in wide-angle view and then down at the large diamonds that were everywhere. He was completely unaware of the massive dark shark head with two glowing intelligent eyes that looked above the surface of the water, stalking him close to the shore. But Bud saw the shark when the explorer looked up again and started to panic.

"There! Look over there!" he yelled at the cell-phone screen as he jumped up and down with a sort of fearful excitement. "Why doesn't the control room see it?" Bud was bewildered.

The Russian just continued along the shore. "There are diamonds everywhere, comrades," he said.

Another swirl, and now a large splash. The shark was now on the move in the water, closing in fast on the Russian's position. The Russian looked up again. The webcam mounted on the helmet of the spacesuit followed the Russian's gaze, looking out on the lake. The video feed showed a very large creature clearly now, moving extremely quickly toward the Russian's position.

Bud yelled again at his cell phone, "Move! Get out of there!"

Now the control-room team saw the large water movement toward the Russian explorer and the glowing eyes of the large creature.

Bud's father lunged forward, "Go! Get out of there!" he yelled into the microphone.

But it was too late.

The Russian was too slow. A massive, sharklike creature with its mouth wide open, revealing large, dagger-sharp teeth and a huge, dark body that Bud figured was at least forty-five feet long and five feet wide.

The creature broke water in a thrust and lunged onto the mud shoreline, closing in on the Russian explorer's position with its jaws open, moving from side to side. Water splashed violently as the large creature thrust its large tail back and forth, half of its body in the water and half on the mud shoreline.

The Russian screamed as the creature closed its jaws, and then suddenly the video stream from the Russian went black before turning to static.

Bud stood in the hallway, watching in shock.

The Russian's vital signs no longer displayed. Static was still displaying on the computer terminal from the Russian's video feed.

"I'm closing in on his position," the American explorer said as he ran toward the shoreline where the Russian had been. She arrived just in time for her video stream to show a sharklike creature working its large tail from side to side away from the shoreline.

"Oh, my—" the American explorer said.

The creature's large muscular body worked itself back into the lake in only a few powerful motions. It quickly dove deep as the lake's surface became still again. Bubbles formed on the surface shortly before the Russian's helmet broke the surface like a fishing bobber. The Russian explorer was gone.

Bud's father yelled, "Return to base! Repeat! Return to base! Get the hell out of there! Now!"

Bud remained frozen with his heart racing as he continued to watch the video stream on his cell phone.

The Australian explorer's video stream showed diamonds scattered over the area. Just as he was collecting samples, he obviously had heard the radio transmission and began struggling in the mud to run. His video was bouncing around frantically as he moved each foot.

Bud yelled at the explorers in the hallway as if he could be heard, "Get out of there!" Bud realized no one could hear him except for confused team members walking by him in the hallway. "I knew it. I just knew there were big creatures down there."

Both explorers moved as fast as they could in the thick mud with their oversized spacesuits toward the transport entrance. The video coming from their webcams bounced up and down.

Bud's father continued to repeat himself as the rustling and panic in the control room grew more intense. "Get the hell out of there, now! People! Move!" He took a breath and then shouted to the people in the control room, "Let's get it together in here. Replay that video feed for me now!"

Bud couldn't believe what he was watching. He remained captivated in the middle of the hallway, looking at his cell phone with his mouth open.

Oblivious to what had just happened to the Russian, the Australian told the American explorer as they walked up the transport ramp, "Holy dooley, mate! Where is Adrian?"

Before the American explorer could answer, Bud's father repeated himself. "Move it! Get out of there! Now!"

The transport video showed the Australian and American explorers throwing themselves against the wall of the transport as the American explorer hit the transport engage button with a punch. Both explorers fell to the floor as the door closed and the transport engaged. Up the transport went, back to the central control center, squealing even more loudly than before.

Bud changed the view on his cell phone to the Mission Control webcam and watched.

"Kurt, what just happened?" Bud's father asked.

Kurt was replaying in slow motion the video showing a very large, sharklike creature closing its jaws on the Russian. He looked at his Australian assistant to answer.

"Quite amazing, sir," the assistant managed. "It appears that there are more than diamonds down there. There also appears to be live, predatory animals that are very big, very dangerous … and apparently very hungry." Kurt's assistant breathed hard, trying to regain his composure.

"I could see that, doggone it!" Bud's father shouted. "I need more information. Let's call an emergency team meeting now. We need to regroup and figure out what the hell happened down there."

Bud could see Kurt on his cell-phone video. Kurt was zooming in on the video feed to enlarge the diamonds on the screen. He appeared to smile.

"What the heck? He's smiling?" Bud said as he watched, still standing frozen in the middle of the hallway.

"And turn off the live Internet feed until we figure this out," Bud's father said. "The entire world just saw one of our team members get eaten by some monster creature of the lake, for God's sake."

Kurt grabbed a phone in the Mission Control room.

Suddenly, Bud remembered where he was going. He looked up, realizing he was still standing in the middle of the hallway.

"OMG!" he said, pronouncing each letter. He began to reflect on what he had just witnessed. He disconnected the transmission, put the cell phone in his pocket, and started running at full speed.

— 32 —

BUD ARRIVED AT HIS room out of breath; he grabbed his oversized backpack with the cell phone containing his video app and all his other equipment before letting Casey out of his kennel. Casey trailed behind as Bud left their living quarters to pick up Peter at the expedition school.

Peter was slowly moving down the hallway, balancing a tall stack of papers on his lap, when Bud arrived out of breath with Casey behind him.

"Thanks for helping me carry these test results," Peter said. "I need them in the control room to compare readings."

Bud just ignored him, grabbing as many papers as he could stuff into his backpack. "We need to get to the Mission Control room pronto. Something big just happened at the lake."

"What happened?"

Bud put on his backpack and jumped on the back of Peter's wheelchair. "Not sure—it happened on my way here. I think an explorer just got eaten. I told you there were creatures down there!"

"What? Are you kidding me? Eaten?"

"Yep. The creature was huge and made the explorer look like a Happy Meal," Bud said. "Let's go."

They were moving at a good speed on Peter's wheelchair, with Bud hanging on the back and Casey trying unsuccessfully to keep up. Peter accelerated toward the Mission Control room.

Casey limped farther behind them, slobbering all over the hallway.

— 33 —

BUD HELD ON TIGHTLY with one hand to the back of Peter's wheelchair and held his cell phone with the other, watching the video feed from the Mission Control webcam they had installed. His grip on both chair and phone became tighter with each corner Peter navigated.

Casey struggled unsuccessfully to keep up, dropping farther and farther behind them.

"Wow, looks like everyone is freaking out," Bud said as Peter's wheelchair came to a sudden stop outside the Mission Control room.

Both the American and Australian scientists had just exited out of the clean room surrounding the transport. Team members were running around everywhere. The scientists took off their helmets and walked out together while talking very animatedly with Bud's father and Kurt.

Suddenly, Bud saw a group of black masked commandos down the hallway behind them, moving quickly with AK-47s toward the Mission Control room. Bud couldn't believe what he was seeing.

"Down, down—get down on knees now!" they shouted, along with a few choice Spanish words that Bud didn't understand, continuing down the hallway.

Bud watched in complete terror as the commandos quickly overpowered the minimally trained security personnel roaming the end of the long hallway, seemingly surrendering their firearms more quickly than a hot potato.

"Quick, Peter!" Bud yelled. "This way!"

"What the—" started Peter, who had not turned around in his wheelchair to see the fast-moving commandos coming their way.

"No time, just move it. Trust me," Bud said.

The boys quickly made their way into the Mission Control room before the commandos arrived and froze against a wall. Casey caught up to them.

"Casey, sit, boy," commanded Bud. "Stay."

Peter started again, "What the heck is going—"

Twenty black masked commandos burst into the Mission Control room, yelling in Spanish and pointing their high-tech weaponry at anyone who moved. Two commandos went straight to the communication backbone and took it offline. The camp was now completely isolated from the outside world. The entire room became silent. Even Casey sat perfectly still, watching. Some of the expedition team members began to cry; another screamed.

"What in the world? What is going on here?" Bud's father demanded.

General Hernandez slowly walked into Mission Control. The shocked team members all around Bud and Peter gave his large, imposing frame their full attention.

Bud recognized the bully general from the news video.

The general puffed on the largest cigar Bud had ever seen, blowing a cloud of smoke toward the ceiling.

He approached Bud's father. "You're the one who was in the press conference. You pig!"

The general put his cigar in his mouth and then pushed Bud's father hard on the chest with his left hand while waving a pistol with his other hand.

Bud's father was knocked back on his heels.

The general took his cigar out of his mouth and blew out a large cloud of smoke.

Bud stood against the wall, frozen with fear, trying to figure out what to do.

"You pigs are no longer welcome on Argentine soil," said the general as he continued waving the loaded pistol at Bud's father. "You're all my prisoners."

"Where the hell is our security?" yelled Bud's father, his voice trembling but still determined.

"Silence, you American trespasser!" the general said in an angry huff as he pushed Bud's father again, this time harder.

Bud noticed Kurt moving toward the general. Kurt picked up the two explorer sample bags and slipped them in his lab coat pockets.

"What's Kurt doing with those bags?" whispered Bud. "Why is he getting so close to the general?"

The general looked at the probe images on the monitors. One image showed a close-up of the large number of diamonds on the ground near what appeared to be the lake.

The general pointed and smiled. "Excelente!" He turned on the expedition camp intercom and began broadcasting to the team around the camp from the control room. "Expedition team, the great country of Argentina has taken our rightful territory back. We're holding you under house arrest until we arrange for your return to your own countries. You must remain in your quarters until further notice." The general took a deep breath. "Do not, I repeat, do *not* underestimate the great power of Argentina, or you will be shot." The general left the microphone on. He was still broadcasting.

Two commandos grabbed Kurt. The general nodded, and the commandos shoved Kurt forward. General Hernandez aimed and fired his gun at Kurt. The sound of the gunshot roared throughout the expedition camp via the intercom as Kurt screamed in pain. The team members in the control room began screaming as the commandos shouted at them in Spanish; more team members began to cry.

The general nodded and smiled. He calmly said, "End transmission."

A commando turned the microphone off.

Bud pulled out the worn picture of himself and his mother. He looked at the picture closely, and then he knew what he needed to do. Bud hated bullies, and this one had to be the worst yet. He put the picture back in his pocket and tapped Peter on the shoulder. It was time to do something.

"Leave the papers here. I'll jump on the back of your wheelchair and we'll make a run for it," he whispered. "We need to call your dad on our backup network."

"On the count of three, let's move." Bud paused. "One ... two ... three!" Bud jumped on the back of Peter's wheelchair and Peter threw down the papers and turned his wheelchair on full power headed toward the door. They quickly accelerated to full speed, but Casey lagged behind them.

The commandos spread themselves around the room, poking people with their guns. Amid the shock of what just occurred, no one had shut the clean-room door leading to the open transport doors. Peter maneuvered quickly around the Mission Control room. He turned hard to avoid a commando and then headed straight into the clean room.

Commandos moved in all directions as Peter concentrated on avoiding a collision. Gunfire rang out, but Peter's wheelchair moved too quickly.

"Hold your fire," yelled the general somewhere behind them. "I want them alive!"

Casey moved awkwardly with determination to keep up with Peter, and amazingly, stayed close behind Peter's wheelchair. Then, with no warning at all, Casey caught up all at once and managed to get in front of Peter. He suddenly jumped up on the wheelchair with a burst of energy that neither Peter nor Bud had expected, landing squarely onto Peter's lap. Casey's momentum carried him hard into the wheelchair controls.

Peter's wheelchair took a sharp right and then accelerated, and Casey fell off the wheelchair. Bud's grip tightened as he almost fell while Peter avoided running into another commando trying to grab them. The wheelchair drove right through the clean room and into the transport elevator. Peter hit the brakes hard to try to avoid hitting the transport back wall.

Bud was thrown off the wheelchair and landed with a thump on his heavy backpack against the inside wall of the transport. He looked around and quickly realized they were both inside the transport. He started to nervously get back on his feet. The commandos suddenly appeared and rushed toward the transport.

"We better—" Just as Bud was helping Peter turn his wheelchair around in the transport, Casey bolted in front of the commandos and into the transport and then jumped onto Peter again.

"Get off, Case!" Peter yelled, pushing Casey off the chair and against the transport sidewall, hitting the large control button on the control panel. Before they could move, the transport doors shut, trapping both boys and Casey inside while the commandos remained outside. The transport began falling rapidly.

"What ... is ... happening?" yelled Bud as he felt his stomach move into his throat.

"Feels like we're going doooown," yelled Peter. "Gooingg tooo faaast ... ssomethiingg wrrrrong ... ahhhhhhhhhh!"

Moments later, *whamp!* The transport came to a screeching halt. The boys had reached lake level.

Smoke billowed from the transport shaft as the control panel went dim. An emergency suction device engaged, sucking the smoke out of the transport.

The doors opened suddenly with a screech and then a loud thud.

Casey panicked, running full speed out of the transport and out of sight.

"Case!" yelled Bud. But Casey was nowhere to be seen.

"I think we're in really big trouble," Peter said as his voice trembled.

Bud gave Peter a blank stare and shook his head. "Unbelievable," said Bud. "What else could go wrong?"

— 34 —

PETER PUSHED EVERY BUTTON on the control panel, but the doors remained open.

"Casey! Casey!" yelled Bud out of the transport door in a loud, raspy whisper. He looked at Peter. "I have to go after him. You stay here."

"Here? Not a chance. I'm not staying here alone," Peter said, fumbling with the controls of his wheelchair after pushing on the transport control panel buttons one last time.

"Okay," Bud agreed nervously. "Let's both go, before Casey gets in more trouble."

Bud grabbed his backpack and walked beside Peter's wheelchair. They moved slowly down the transport's cement ramp until they reached ground level.

"Casey! Casey!" called out Bud with his hands cupped around his mouth. For the first time, Bud began to look around in amazement. "Holy cow!" he said as he looked above him at the glowing light show.

The shimmering blue glowing algae overhead slowly changed color in bright bursts, creating purple, blue, and white patterns that flowed above the lake. Bright white glowing butterflies floated all around them. Glowing insects buzzed as they chased other insects. Some glowed bright white; others glowed neon shades of yellow, blue, green, and red. The colors were bright and vibrant. Different colors of light were everywhere.

"This place is amazing," Peter said. "Light is not only coming from above, but from those plants and butterflies all around us. They're generating light, too."

Bud focused back on his missing dog. "Casey," shouted Bud. They continued to move slowly after leaving the transport ramp. Bud walked carefully next to Peter, staying close to his wheelchair.

A few yards from the ramp, high white grasses made it difficult to move as they swept across the boys' path. Off in the distance, squeals, roars, splashes, and other noises became clearer to Bud as he listened for Casey's bark. Bud moved large, glowing bushes out of the way of Peter's wheelchair as they continued to slowly navigate farther away from the ramp.

"Casey!" shouted Bud again.

Peter maneuvered his wheelchair over the white grasses and through light mud, small rocks, scattered diamonds, and large, glowing, white-leafed plants.

"Casey is nowhere to be seen, Bud," Peter said as they moved farther away from the transport ramp. "This is not cool. We should go back. Maybe Casey—"

Suddenly, a white body with a large, dark wingspan and glowing eyes flew directly at them. Bud ducked low to the ground in a jerking motion and moved as close to Peter's wheelchair as possible to avoid a collision with the fast-moving creature.

Peter began to stutter. "This is b-bad ... really bad."

Quivering, Bud said, "Man, that was close. That thing looked like a vampire bat."

"Did you see those huge, glowing eyes? It looked like it could see right through us!"

"Yeah, great," Bud said. "Next thing we'll see is a werewolf. Great ... just great." Bud lifted his head slightly, looking straight up, sweat pouring into his eyes. The creature hovered above their position. "Uh-oh," Bud whispered. "Look up."

Bud got a closer look at the creature. It looked like a cross between a blackbird, a huge firefly, and ... well, a mouse with glowing eyes. It let out a loud squeal and flapped its large dark wings, as if threatening them.

"Think we can make a run for it?" Bud said, looking at Peter with wide eyes.

"Maybe you can," Peter said.

For the first time, Bud realized that the wheelchair was not a help, but a hindrance. Bud took a breath in frustration and leaned back to look up again. This time he didn't see the flying creature hovering above them anymore. He saw a bully hovering above them ... and Bud hated bullies.

The hovering creature let out another loud squeal directly overhead, flapping its large wings while its white tail feathers acted as a rudder. Even its feathers glowed. It let out yet another squeal, this time louder, just as a large clump of smelly poop fell smack-dab on Bud's shoes.

"Aw, jeez. Really? Really? Are you kidding me?" Bud looked up at the bully creature in disgust.

"Ooooh, yuck," Peter said. "Good thing you leaned back, dude." He grinned.

"That's it, Mr. Pooping Bully Bird Vampire Creature!" Bud shot straight up in a burst, like a piston, with his arms moving around wildly as he let out a deep burst of air and yelled, "Rah rah, beat it, bully!"

The creature squealed again but this time took off like a rocket.

Peter looked at Bud with a stare. Bud stared right back at Peter. "So much for pooping vampires," Bud said with a certain swagger.

"Yeah, but looks like he left something behind," Peter said with a nervous chuckle as he looked at the muck still on Bud's feet.

Bud wiped his feet on the tall, white grass and then looked around. He noticed he could see the lake in the distance through the heavy vegetation. "Check that out, Peter—there's the lake."

"Just get me b-back to the transport," Peter said with a slight stutter. "Please, I'm totally freaking out here."

Bud helped Peter get back to the transport ramp, where Peter felt more comfortable. "Get inside the transport, and I'll go find Casey," Bud said as he looked down at what appeared to be very large footprints in the mud.

"Use one of your video dragonflies," pleaded Peter. "That way, you can stay here with me."

"Good idea. Let me give that a whirl." Bud took out his cell phone and a dragonfly robot. He tapped a few buttons on his cell phone. "Here goes nothing." Bud activated the dragonfly, and its wings started moving rapidly and buzzing loudly. Soon it was hovering one foot from the ground.

"Let me see. Can you bring it over here?" asked Peter.

Bud stood by the side of Peter's wheelchair and started maneuvering the dragonfly as he tapped on his cell phone.

The video was working, and Bud was using the video from the dragonfly to help him fly it.

Up it went, higher and higher. Bud tapped on his cell phone to command it to hover above them and then rotated it 360 degrees with its camera pointed slightly downward. The view was amazing, with glowing vegetation everywhere.

"Where could Case be? Let me maneuver this …" Bud continued. He tapped the phone a few more times, and the dragonfly flew toward the lake, now almost out of sight from the boys' position on the transport ramp. But the video coming from the dragonfly robot and displaying on Bud's cell phone looked sharp.

Suddenly Bud could see that same pooping vampire who had buzzed their heads flying directly toward the dragonfly. "Uh-oh!" In an instant, the flying creature closed in on the dragonfly.

The video went black and then came back on again as it fell to the ground.

Bud and Peter both jumped.

"Holy cats, did you see that?" Bud asked. "It tried to eat our dragonfly, but then apparently spit it out."

"Probably realized it wasn't flesh and blood, or something."

"I didn't see Case anywhere. I need to find him. I'm really worried."

"Okay, but be please careful."

Bud put on his backpack and walked slowly down the ramp, jumping and twisting from side to side at each strange sound he heard.

After struggling in the mud, Bud finally reached the lakeshore. Out of breath, he stopped to examine his surroundings. Casey was nowhere around.

"Casey, where the heck did you go?" Bud was trembling.

Bud looked out over the shimmering lake. Colors and white sparkles reflected off its surface for as far as he could see.

"What the heck?" Bud said. He saw the helmet with a Russian flag on the visor bobbing on the lake.

A glowing light from above distracted Bud. It started as a small streak, waving ever so slightly, changing in color within the lake biosphere. The light quickly grew and stretched as far as the eye could see, flowing like a giant, brightly colored sheet in a summer wind. The light shone incredibly bright and then dimmed and repeated, illuminating the plant life growing around the lake with a white, red, orange, and blue glow.

"I need to get back to the transport. This place is nuts," Bud said as he started to backtrack as fast as he could manage.

White glowing creatures the size of butterflies, floated all around, landing on his head and shoulders and then flying off when he moved. They flew among the colorful glowing plants that were everywhere.

"Casey!" Bud said as loudly as he dared. Bud remembered he had a cell phone in his backpack that could communicate with Peter's wheelchair. He quickly retrieved the cell phone from his backpack and then tapped on it, enabling a wifi link to Peter's wheelchair computer.

"Hello?" Peter said.

"Peter, I still don't see Case. Everything seems to be glowing. This place is nuts. I'm starting to—" Bud stopped. "Uh-oh." Panic overtook him.

"What's wrong, Bud?"

Splash, swoosh, splash, swoosh.

Bud looked to his right and whispered quickly with excitement, "Holy cow! A huge glowing creature twice the size of a hippo is feeding on the tall grasses and what looks like glowing mulberry leaves. Everything glows around this place, and that creature has got to weigh five thousand pounds, Peter. It has green glowing skin that seems to provide a guide light as it feeds." Bud tried to catch his breath as he noticed the creature resembled a modern-day water buffalo, but with a glowing, massive body and large horns. "I knew it! I knew it! It's huge. I wish my Dad were here. We need to get out of here, now—" Bud disconnected the phone and started running, startling the large creature for a moment. It looked in Bud's direction and then ignored him.

Bud stumbled over large diamonds that lay everywhere, reflecting a rainbow of colors. He fell to his knees with a thump.

"Ouch! Casey, where are you?" He took a breath and slowly got back to his feet. He called out to Casey again.

"Umph!" He tripped and fell again. This time, Bud stayed low to the ground as he got his bearings and wiped the mud from his hands. He saw a herd of small creatures off in the distance away from the lake, with what looked to be a few larger creatures around the perimeter of the small herd.

He turned his attention back to the large creature moving closer toward him, but it completely ignored Bud as it feasted on the white grasses along the lakeshore, wandering farther away from the herd in the background.

Bud was just about to run again when he saw bushes near the creature move. He peeked over the grasses slowly.

"Oh, my," Bud gulped when he saw a large, dark, evil-looking, catlike creature moving along the shoreline, stalking the large buffalolike creature feeding on the grass. Bud froze.

The creature looked similar to a large cat at well over one thousand pounds, but with slick, gray skin. The creature's color changed from gray to an orange glow and then back to gray as it approached the large grazing creature. Its head and neck had the only fur, which was bright yellow and black; the hair looked similar to a large collar around its large, dark, slick head. If Bud weren't so frightened, he might have thought the creature looked as if it should have been a cartoon, as the creature's changing colors and fur combination were almost comical—although it did have an evil look to it that caused Bud to take it seriously.

The creature crouched down as it stalked the buffalolike creature still moving closer to Bud. Bud saw the crouched creature's round, bright yellow eyes lock onto the green glowing buffalo creature in an intense stare. It was still getting closer to it. Bud held his breath and tried not to make a sound.

The catlike creature picked up one front and back paw simultaneously. Both its legs lifted large, deadly paws in slow motion, shifting its weight while moving forward. Then the other two legs moved forward as the creature's large body remained crouched low to the ground.

The buffalolike creature still did not hear the evil-looking cat creature approaching. It lifted its nose, as if to smell a strange scent in the air. It sniffed again.

Bud started to shake as he held his breath, watching but not wanting to move.

Suddenly, the creature turned with a jerk to the right, and then to the left. Bud could see fear radiating from the large buffalolike creature as it glowed brighter. It lunged forward, nearly stepping on Bud. Its massive body moved slowly at first and then picked up speed as it moved away from the lake.

It took several seconds for the huge creature to get up to speed as its head, shoulders, and legs struggled to move its massive body.

The sinister catlike creature threw itself forward and was now in full pursuit of the buffalolike creature. It roared as its frustration increased while it struggled to catch its prey. Both creatures were now far enough away from Bud to give Bud the confidence to carefully stand up to watch.

The buffalolike creature was at full speed now, moving quickly toward the thick jungle. It looked as if the buffalo creature were about to escape as it looked back to see the cat creature slowing down.

That was close, thought Bud as the adrenaline pumped through his veins. He watched as the buffalo creature quickly approached the jungle.

Then a loud bellow echoed across the lake, causing a large number of flying vampire creatures to scatter into the air. A second cat creature took down the massive buffalo creature. It was clearly in pain.

Bud cringed as he watched.

A dark orange, glowing hue lit up the area around the buffalo creature. It bellowed again.

Bud started talking to himself nervously. "A roar from the same direction, but that roar clearly came from another—OMG!" He tried to run, but his feet moved as if they were in molasses due to the thick mud. Bud struggled to catch his breath, realizing the roar was getting closer to his position.

Another roar—this time even closer to Bud. Bud ran faster. Out of the corner of Bud's eye, he saw the large, wide paws of another cat creature quickly moving toward him.

It roared again, and then multiple cat creatures roared together, echoing around the lake. A dark-orange glow grew bright all around Bud as he ran with determination. He ran as hard as he could in the mud, using all his strength to pull one foot away from the ground at a time. Finally, he was close to the ramp.

"Peter, Peter! We need to get out of here, now!" yelled Bud.

"Did you hear all those noises?" Peter said from his wheelchair on the ramp.

"Get in the transport! *Now!*"

Bud heard a growl in the bushes that sounded close—very close, in fact. Too close. *GGRRRRLLLL.* It was loud, with a low-pitched rumble, and getting closer.

The large plants jerked to the side as three sets of large, yellow, glowing eyes peered through the white leaves. More growling came from the bushes, growing louder.

Bud realized the cat creatures had followed him.

"Oh, no," Bud said, looking around and realizing there was no place for them to go.

The boys, beginning to panic, backed up slowly toward the transport.

The cat creature growled loudly as it moved its large, dark, muscular body slowly out of the bushes, stalking the boys. It methodically moved each leg, slowly moving toward the boys, fully exposed. The growl turned into a roar as the large animal displayed its huge, swordlike teeth and thick, hungry, drooling tongue.

"It … it … it's gi-gi-gigantic," stammered Bud. He started to shake as he took out his picture of his mother and held it closely and then whispered, "I need you, Mom." Bud took a deep breath, looking for the strength he needed to protect Peter and himself.

Peter noticed Bud's picture and put his arm up on Bud's shoulder and squeezed. Bud was sure they were goners.

Suddenly the creature lunged at them and roared like a lion. Bud reacted instantly, putting the picture away as he jumped in front of Peter's wheelchair in a fighting stance with his eyes closed, ready to protect Peter, like Spider-Man.

"Bud!" yelled Peter.

Just as the cat creature was about to reach them, diamond-tipped wooden spears came from nowhere, flying from all directions toward the cat creatures.

Swh, swh, swh. Thump, thump, thump. The cat creatures roared in pain as more spears dug deeply into their flesh. Each creature twisted and turned in pain as it collapsed and then jerked in a violent motion.

Bud opened his eyes and felt a slight pinch on his neck, sort of like a mosquito bite.

"Ouch!" "Ow!" Both Bud and Peter slapped their necks at nearly the same time, brushing off the small poisonous sticks that had struck their necks.

Finally, the roars became silent as the three catlike creatures came to rest just six feet from them. Bud fell down into a sitting position. He couldn't move and was somehow frozen sitting up, but he could still breathe and talk.

"Peter," Bud cried out.

"I'm okay. Behind you. Can't move."

"Me neither," replied Bud.

The bushes moved out of the way, revealing a group of what Bud thought looked like medium-sized dolphinlike creatures with thick arms and legs wearing loose, dark leather clothes, walking toward them slowly.

"Walking dolphins with arms and hands? Peter, are you seeing this? I've got to be dreaming."

"I see them," Peter said as his voice trembled.

Each one of the group had a bow arched with an arrow. Leather straps secured shiny, diamond-tipped spears to their shoulders and other handheld weapons around their waists. They appeared to glide slowly toward the boys as they moved. These creatures wore headbands and necklaces of colorful jewels intermingled with shells and what appeared to be large, extracted dagger teeth. As they came closer, Bud thought they looked like the human version of a dolphin, only larger and more muscular than Bud.

Bud observed each had large, inviting eyes with long eyelashes, and short, stubby gray noses above their small mouths, which appeared to be frozen in a friendly half smile. Their heads were smooth, gray, and hairless. Thick shoulders flowed into short, muscular arms and oversized hands; short legs flowed into extra-large feet that were covered with dark leather boots that were laced up each leg.

The dolphin creatures worked together to quickly secure the massive catlike creatures and carried them off. Bud still couldn't move, but he realized these dolphinlike creatures had just saved them from being the cats' next meal.

Bud tried again to move his legs and then his arms. Nothing. Bud felt as if he were entirely paralyzed, yet he was still sitting upright.

Two of the dolphin creatures looked curiously at Bud and Peter, hesitating at first, and then picked up Peter from his wheelchair, leaving his wheelchair behind. Another creature looked carefully at Bud and sniffed, then picked up Bud as smoothly and easily as if he were a sack of potatoes.

Bud was amazed at the lack of hesitation as these dolphinlike creatures moved smoothly in almost synchronized movements, each seemingly knowing exactly where to go and what to do. Bud could hear clicking sounds, low hums, and tones forming what Bud thought were words, but they sounded like gibberish to him. He knew they were communicating, but he could not understand them.

One dolphinlike creature who was somewhat larger than the rest of the group directed the group. Bud figured he was probably the leader. They carried Bud and Peter into the large-leaved bushes and glowing brush. Bud still trembled but felt more relaxed now, almost as if his eyelids weighed one hundred pounds. A warm feeling flowed through his body and calmness came over him as he realized the small darts that had landed in their necks must have carried some sort of calming agent along with a sedative.

Bud's eyelids became even heavier, and a wave of exhaustion came over him. Time slowed down. Bud looked at Peter being carried in front of him and tried unsuccessful to reach out to him.

Bud blacked out.

— 35 —

Bud woke up with a shock to see one of the dolphin creatures sitting directly in front of him and staring. The creature looked like a child compared to the others. Its skin was a softer, smoother gray, and its features were smaller. Its large, soft, friendly eyes looked closely at Bud and blinked slowly, as if studying him.

Bud cleared his throat. "Who are you?"

The creature turned its head slightly to the right, as if trying to understand him, and continued staring at Bud. Bud pointed to himself and said very slowly, "Bud."

The creature gave Bud a nod. It pointed to itself and made a series of clicks and tones.

Bud made a face. "I do not understand."

The creature appeared to understand Bud's frustration. It tried again. This time it pointed to itself and slowly pronounced, "Te-ko," with a clicking sound combined with tones.

Bud got it.

The creature then pointed to a few of the other creatures who were standing around Peter and said "Te-ko" each time it pointed to one of the dolphin creatures.

"I get it!" Bud said. "You're the Teko." He gestured to indicate the entire group all at once.

The creature's soft eyes opened wide, and its natural smile grew larger.

"Where is my friend?" Bud said.

But the little Teko formed what looked to be claw shapes with its hands and made a roaring clicking tone sound. Then slowly pronounced, "Ki-ta."

Bud nodded again. He understood. The catlike creatures that nearly killed them back at the transport were called kita.

The creature then pointed to where Peter was lying motionless. It then made a series of hand motions reassuring Bud that Peter was okay.

The little Teko then made a big, round motion with its arms, getting Bud's full attention and said, "Be-so." It reenacted how the kita had killed the beso that Bud had witnessed.

Bud grew more nervous and tried again to communicate with the creature. "My name is Bud. What is yours?"

The young Teko gave Bud a puzzled look. Bud asked again, this time using hand signals and speaking much more slowly.

"What is your name?"

The Teko grinned and then made a series of clicks, as if it were laughing. The Teko replied in high-pitched clicks and low tones and hoots, almost singing.

"kkk ccc kkck ckkc kkcc hooc ckk."

"Sure, like I can say that," Bud said as he rolled his eyes, shaking his head. Bud pointed at the creature and said, "Little One. I will call you Little One."

Little One just looked at Bud curiously.

"We come from above." Bud pointed at himself and then motioned upward. Little One looked perplexed, but nodded. Bud was scared, yet he remained relaxed, presumably from the sedative delivered by the dart in his neck.

Bud turned his attention to where Peter lay; Bud's friend was starting to move now. Bud saw a group of Teko touching and massaging Peter. Their hands glowed yellow as they moved quickly over Peter's legs.

They had sad looks on their faces at first while working on Peter. Peter's face glowed light red, almost pink, but he remained unconscious.

Bud stood up quickly and wobbled toward Peter.

"Hey, what's going on? What are you doing to my friend?"

Using more hand motions, Little One reassured Bud that they were trying to help Peter, gently patting Bud as the group continued to work on Peter.

Bud stayed out of the way and watched.

Peter began to wake up. "Hey, what the—Bud? Bud? Where are you?" stammered Peter as he wiggled around, trying to lift his head.

"Peter, I'm over here. I'm okay," Bud said, watching the Teko continue to rub Peter's legs.

"What are they doing?" Peter asked.

"They're trying to help you, Peter."

Bud noticed a colorful, glowing butterfly floating gracefully around Peter. It slowly moved its large green and blue glowing wings in what looked like a dance.

"Look, Bud—a butterfly. It's beautiful," Peter said as he pointed to it. Then he did a double take at the Teko. "They're not scary looking at all."

"I don't think they want to hurt us. After all, they did save our lives."

"Hey, my legs are starting to tingle," Peter said.

A Teko gave Peter something to drink in a cup that looked like pottery of some sort. It motioned for Peter to drink. Peter reluctantly took a sip. "Hmm, not bad. Kind of tastes like warm fruit punch," Peter said, licking his lips.

The Teko continued to work on Peter's legs and lower back. Their soft touch seemed to keep Peter at ease. Their dolphinlike facial characteristics made them look as if they were constantly smiling at Peter, and their eyes were soft and friendly.

Peter wiggled his toes, and then his feet, and then his legs. "Hey, I can move my legs," Peter said, somewhat perplexed. "They feel stronger."

Five Teko kept working around Peter. They stood Peter up before continuing to rub and massage his legs and lower back with their fast-moving, glowing hands. They gave Peter more to drink.

One Teko looked older than the rest and wore a long headdress made of feathers. A necklace of leather and large jewels was displayed prominently around his neck. He sounded as if he were humming as he rubbed a clear crystal attached to a long, white bone on Peter's legs. The crystal glowed light blue as it touched Peter's legs.

Bud smelled something cooking nearby. It smelled like the mesquite barbecue his family used to have each summer when his mother was alive.

A young Teko brought Bud a bowl of what appeared to be soup. Thinly sliced pieces of meat, strange-looking vegetables, and white leaves floating in a broth. A large, doughy substance floated in the soup as well. At first Bud didn't want to try it, but Little One insisted. Bud took a small sip and then another.

It tasted like a beef broth with carrots and had a sweet aftertaste. The doughy substance also had a creamy, sweet taste and quickly dissolved in his mouth.

"Hey, this is good," Bud said. He gulped it down, using the wooden bowl as a large cup, slurping the soup and smacking his lips.

Little One smiled and then gave Bud a different drink.

"Hey, this tastes like apple juice," Bud said as he burped unexpectedly. "Whoops, sorry."

Little One appeared to smile at Bud.

Bud heard a bark. It was Casey. Casey ran over to Bud and began licking Bud all over his face. Bud, who could now move normally again, hugged Casey.

"Casey! Thank goodness you're okay! Good boy, good boy." Bud's eyes filled with tears at the sight of his dog. "It's so good to see you, Case."

Casey ran around like a young puppy, jumping up and down in a complete circle."

"Peter, Casey is jumping around like Tigger. You know, in the Winnie the Pooh stories?"

"Yeah, I know who Tigger is," Peter said as he made a face. Peter stretched, but still appeared to move cautiously.

The Teko appeared to be done working on him, and Peter, who looked exhausted, lay down and quickly fell asleep.

Bud relaxed. It looked as if he, Peter, and Casey were going to be fine now, thanks to the Teko. Little One handed him a piece of meat.

"It tastes like a barbecued rib. This is great," Bud said to Little One. He gave a small amount to Casey, who begged for more.

Bud quickly made friends with Little One. For the first time since waking up, he started to look around and realized they were in some sort of cave with wooden lanterns hanging everywhere, projecting a glowing yellow light that reflected throughout the cave.

Little One motioned to Bud to follow him.

"What about Peter?" Bud asked slowly, using as many hand motions as he could think of.

Little One motioned to Bud that it would be okay to leave Peter and made hand signals that Peter needed much rest now, putting his hands near his face and closing his eyes to mimic sleep. He then motioned for Bud to follow him. Casey darted out ahead of Bud reaching Little One first.

As Bud followed Little One, he quickly realized the main cave extended farther underground through many long passageways extending into other cave sections. Everywhere Bud went glowed yellow like candlelight, but Bud was sure the wooden lanterns weren't lit by candles; something appeared to move inside them. Each lantern was a glowing box made from thick, dark wood and white grasses. Bud stopped and inspected the glowing box. He opened the top and jumped as a large group of entrapped fireflies flew into his face all at once as they escaped.

"Ingenious," Bud whispered.

Bud looked closer at the cave's features as he followed Little One farther into the cave. The cave's spectacular diamond formations shimmered and glowed with a golden sparkle. Bud could tell by the texture of the cave walls that they were very old. Ancient stalactites grew downward from above, with colorful gems embedded in the white formations. Many ancient drawings of animals and plants covered the walls.

"So these caves keep you safe, don't they?" Bud said as he realized the importance of the caves to the Teko.

Little One ignored him and kept walking.

Bud saw Teko everywhere, each of whom was busy doing specific tasks. Some were cooking; some were building small wooden and metal mechanical devices; some were working in what looked to be a laboratory, where substances were mixed and combined in boiling metal pots; and some were making clothes.

Bud noticed as they walked through the passages and into different cave sections that each of the Teko in those cave sections appeared focused on a specific task. In one of the smaller sections, there were small Teko—smaller than Little One—being tended to by a number of adult Teko, who sang in high-pitched clicks and tones. They sounded like an orchestra of harmonizing violins.

In some cave sections were beds made with a silky, soft weave and fixtures intricately woven from vines or carved from the bark of trees, painted with artistic patterns and colors.

Little One showed Bud where his tribe cooked in another smaller section, where heat rose from far below; Bud thought it probably came from volcanic vents. Steam and smoke were captured by other vents and disappeared. The Teko made flat loaves of bread from the seeds they had gathered around the lake. Their handiwork included long, crunchy sticks of baked dough and small pieces that looked like breakfast cereal.

The Teko caves were like mazes, with passageways twisting and turning. One could easily get lost in them,

Bud thought. Air flowed through many of the sections; some of the air was warm, some extremely cold. The Teko appeared to have redirected the air to provide their home with the air flow and the warmth they desired. Little One used hand motions to indicate to Bud that certain passageways were dangerous, shaking his head and spreading his fingers in front of himself defensively.

Bud saw an entrance to a passageway blocked by what looked to be very old rocks, stacked nearly four feet high, arranged in the form of a wall blocking the entrance. There were symbols he didn't understand along the top of the wall. Bud was curious.

"Can we get into there?" Bud asked, making a motion toward the blocked entrance.

Little One shook his head no and made a series of serious clicking sounds and low tones, moving his large hands to indicate that they should keep moving.

"I get it, I get it. That one is off-limits."

Little One took Bud and Casey up a long passageway leading out of the caves. Bud saw a huge area cleared of trees. Rows of light-leaved plants intermingled with round, hard-shelled fruit that grew from vines, lined up uniformly in straight lines for as far as the eye could see, surrounded by what looked to Bud to be a fence. Bud realized this was where the Teko grew their food.

Bud did a double take as Casey ran around in circles around them, bounding around more quickly than he had in years, managing to stay close to Bud despite his brisk pace. He was acting like a puppy again. Bud thought Casey looked younger now, with a lot less drool.

Bud noticed there were Teko everywhere, as if they were standing guard. He thought about Peter and wondered how his friend was doing. Bud used hand signs to Little One, trying to communicate that he wanted to return to Peter.

Little One understood and took Bud back to Peter.

"Peter! You're standing!" Bud said when he again saw his friend, who rubbed at his eyes, having clearly just woken up.

Casey jumped up on Peter, almost knocking him down, and then ran over to a group of young Teko and started to play with them.

Peter started to take a step and then another. "Wow! I can ... I can walk!" Peter said. He wobbled and then got his balance. "Hey, I can walk! I can really walk! And my breathing feels ... well, great! I thought it was all a dream, but it wasn't!" Peter shouted.

The Teko had returned to work on Peter with their glowing hands as Peter took each step slowly.

Peter shook his head. He was now walking—well, sort of wobbling—but his legs were working again. Bud watched in disbelief as Peter walked around the glowing cave. Peter's walk was getting more stable by the second.

"How did they do that?" Bud asked Peter.

"They have some pretty cool healing medicines, I guess," replied Peter.

Little One motioned for Peter to stay to get more rest and for Bud to follow him.

"I'll be back," Bud said. "You need to rest now. I think he wants to show me around more while you recover."

"Okay. I'm feeling a little weak, now that I think about it." But to Bud, Peter appeared to be growing stronger. "It's been a long time since I was able to get around without my wheelchair," Peter said with a smile.

Bud waved to Peter and then realized Little One was moving quickly away from him.

"I see Little One's quick-moving tour continues," Bud said.

Casey stayed behind to play with the group of young Teko. He seemed to be quite content at the moment, so Bud ran to catch up with Little One.

— 36 —

BUD LOOKED CAREFULLY AT the tools and weapons the Teko had made from resources around the lake. The Teko had also manufactured what appeared to be metal tools for farming and hunting, which were configured with intricate levers and crude-looking mechanical springs.

Little One was determined to take Bud back to the lake area to show him something. Little One made rapid hand gestures, indicating it was important that Bud go with him. Bud was nervous and reluctant to go at first, but he decided to go anyway.

On the way, Bud was able to get a good look at a hippo-sized creature feeding on the tall grasses near the shoreline. Little One pointed and slowly pronounced, "He-kk-o."

The hekko was feeding on plants near the lake. Its skin was a brown color with purplish glowing hues. Its hide was virtually hairless and appeared moistened by what Bud thought looked like gross mucous glands secreting a bluish neon liquid. Four stubby legs supported the barrel-like bulk of its body as it sloshed slowly through the shallow water near the lake's edge while it fed.

Bud was amazed. Even though they were fifty yards away, the animal appeared massive. It sort of looked like the beso he had seen earlier, but it was much, much larger.

"That creature's gotta weigh sixteen thousand pounds!" Bud said. "Man, it must need to feed constantly on the plants and grasses along the shoreline of the lake."

Little One just looked away as Bud realized he didn't understand what Bud was saying.

The large-leaved plants shimmered and sparkled in the purple light. Bud watched in wonder; the plants were generating their own white light. Sweeping white grasses surrounded the lake, growing close together with the large-leaved plants. The grasses were moving side to side ever so slightly in the warm breeze. The air felt tropical, thick, and humid, with a fine rain falling gently onto Bud. Bud smiled as he inhaled through his nose deeply; the air smelled fresh.

A small splash startled the hekko; its eyes and nostrils protruded slightly out of the water while the rest of its body remained submerged. Another batlike creature was flying overhead and let out a cry.

Little One pointed and said, "Be-to."

Bud remembered that creature from when he had first arrived at the lake. How could he forget? After all, it had tried—and succeeded—to poop on his shoes.

"Hey, he's the one who tried to eat my dragonfly!" Bud said to Little One, who just kept on walking. Bud looked out on the lake and saw a swirl around the dark top of a large creature gliding in the lake as its large dorsal fin broke the surface of the water. More splashes.

Little One pointed. "Ti-ga." Little One made a series of clicks and tones. Bud didn't understand what the clicks and tones meant, but he knew Little One was warning Bud about that creature.

Just then the hekko panicked, looking around in all directions. The beto circled above and squealed again loudly, as if to tell the hekko that danger was close.

Little One stopped and pointed to the hekko. Bud watched.

The hekko started to move its massive frame and stubby legs in an attempt to get out of the lake shallows. The water splashed in all directions as the hekko moaned a low-pitched grunt, desperately grabbing for the safety of the shoreline. After dragging its massive body forward, it quickly moved away from the lake. It had gotten away.

"That was a close one," Bud said.

Little One grabbed Bud's arm and pulled him in the direction of the lakeshore. After a few minutes of walking, they arrived at a small cave entrance, where there were a small number of Teko.

Little One grabbed a box at the cave entrance that gave off light, and Bud followed him deep into the cave. Little One finally stopped, held the light to the cave wall, and gestured for Bud to look.

Bud took a close look. "What? Human figures?" An image on the wall showed human-looking people. Bud couldn't believe what he was seeing. "These drawings show humans ... how can that be?" Bud asked.

Little One smiled, making a number of hand gestures. He pointed at Bud, and then to the wall, and then back at Bud. He almost sounded as if he were giggling.

"But what does this mean?" Bud asked. "Are there humans down here?" Bud pointed at himself and asked the question again with a series of hand motions directed at Little One.

Now Little One appeared to understand. He shook his head with a frown, pointing at Bud and then to the wall.

Bud snapped a quick picture with his cell phone as he realized Little One was trying to tell him that there were no humans here anymore and that these drawings were very, very old and sacred to the Teko. Bud wanted more time to look at the drawings and take more pictures, but Little One would have none of that; he pulled Bud away and took his light, so Bud would follow him out of the cave.

"Guess it is time to go already. Jeez."

The outside light had faded; its purplish hue appeared to be dimming. They headed back to the main Teko caves. Little One took out what appeared to be a square wooden flashlight from a leather satchel he wore around his waist. Little One pressed a section of the wood, and a bright yellow light illuminated from the device.

Bud looked at it closely, trying to figure out how it was built. "This looks like a flashlight … but why is it yellow?" mumbled Bud as he looked closer at it. Bud couldn't resist; he had to know how it worked. He interrupted Little One's tour.

"Little One?" Bud pointed to the wooden flashlight and shrugged.

Little One smiled and untied the two dry vines holding the two sides of the flashlight together. It opened, revealing its contents: three polished, shiny stones. One stone looked like copper, and Bud thought one stone might be zinc. Each stone was separated by pieces of something similar to a gooey cotton glob. Two strands of metal had been shaped into what looked like wire and connected to a rock that looked like a shiny, metallic crystal that gave off the yellow light.

"Aha!" Bud said. "This rock generates the light, sort of like the battery Larry showed me how to make back home. Except … this one rock is different." Bud looked closely at the rock that appeared to be a crystal. "These rocks are the battery, and instead of using a lightbulb, it uses this crystal to generate the light—sort of like the cat whisker, like my dad said. Cool!"

Little One reassembled the wooden flashlight, tied on the two vines holding it all together, and then pressed a small section of the wood. The light reappeared this time, even brighter than before. Bud looked off into the distance and realized that the surrounding mountains appeared to be giving off a similar light, and it reflected off of the ice dome above. Bud looked around again and realized Little One's light wasn't brighter; it was actually getting darker all around them.

Little One became serious again and gestured for Bud to follow him. Bud thought Little One must be warning him that it was dangerous to be out after dark. He picked up the pace.

They both walked quickly back to the caves, where the Teko clan appeared to be preparing to sleep. The yellow glow coming from hundreds of lanterns was much dimmer now compared to when Bud and Little One had left the caves.

Little One brought Bud back to where Peter was lying down and awake.

"How are you feeling?" asked Bud.

"Good. Just really tired. But I'm feeling good," Peter said as he struggled to keep his eyes open.

Little One gestured for Bud to sleep now. Bud wasn't going to debate with Little One, as he was feeling very tired, too, but he wasn't sure he could sleep.

"Case! Oh, there you are, Casey," Bud said as he realized Casey was already beside him, curled up fast asleep. "Thank you for the tour, Little One. There are so many things I want to ask you," Bud said softly. "I was wondering if we could return to the transport when Peter is stronger?" Bud pointed to where he thought the transport was and made some hand motions to try and communicate what he was saying to Little One, pointing at the sky with a whooshing motion. He yawned.

Little One nodded and then lay down next to Peter, motioning for Bud to lie down next to him.

"Peter, when we get back to the transport," Bud whispered, "if it's still not working, we can tap into the communication hardline on the transport and connect the wireless router I have in my backpack. We might be able to communicate with Sara. She still has one of the cell phones we configured."

Peter didn't move. He was already fast asleep.

— 37 —

Bud opened his eyes suddenly as he realized he had fallen asleep. Peter was still sleeping soundly, with Casey curled up beside him. Little One was putting on what looked to be layers of clothing and numerous weapons that hung over both shoulders with leather straps.

"Where are you going?" asked Bud.

Little One ignored Bud and continued putting on more layers.

Bud walked in front of Little One. "I go with you," Bud said using his hands as he spoke.

Little One shook his head no at first, but Bud insisted. Little One finally agreed. "Eg-wa," pronounced Little One slowly, making his hand swim through the air like a fish. Little One turned and walked quickly out of the room.

Bud had to run to keep up with him. "Jeez, you walk fast. Haven't you ever heard of a leisurely stroll?"

They quickly approached the lake. When they arrived, Bud noticed what looked like a small wooden dock and four sleek canoes made out of shiny black wood. Other older Teko were climbing into the canoes.

"Oh … water … ah, lake? Hmm, on second thought, I think I will go see how Peter is feeling," Bud said as he started to turn around and walk away from the lake.

One of the elder Teko grabbed Bud's arm firmly and made a series of clicks and pointed to the canoes.

"Looks like I'm going on a boat ride." Bud got into the same canoe as Little One and grabbed a paddle.

They all paddled together in the sleek wooden canoe. Bud did his best to synchronize his paddling with everyone else's in the canoe. Two muscular Teko warriors paddled with power, their hairless, smooth, muscular, light-gray skin shimmering with each stroke of the paddle in front of Bud. Little One sat behind Bud, steering.

Each stroke caused the Teko's muscular arms and shoulders to contract, flexing their muscles as their heads and short, snub noses did not move atop their thick muscular necks. The Teko warriors paddled with determination, focusing on each stroke of the paddle.

Two Teko warriors paddled in a second canoe close by. The Teko in Bud's canoe slowed the canoe and positioned a glowing, algae-lined trap in the water. The trap made a small vibration when it entered the water that Bud couldn't figure out.

"It must attract something to come to the surface of the water," Bud said to himself.

Little One gave Bud a look and made a sound—*sssst*—as he poked Bud in the back.

"Jeez, you're like the dog whisperer," Bud said under his breath as he realized he needed to be quiet. "Sorry."

Bud saw a school of large, salmon-sized fish in the clear lake water approaching the surface. They moved toward the trap. Little One whispered from behind Bud,

"Eg-wa," and pointed. Suddenly, the egwa broke the surface in a coordinated, neon-blue splash of color.

Whoosh, wammp—two muscular Teko closed the water trap, and six egwa were caught. As their bodies flopped and twisted, their large jaws and interlocking teeth opened and closed frantically. The creatures struggled to break loose as the excited hunting party moved about in the canoe.

"Wicked cool." Bud's eyes were as big as saucers. "Those egwa will make a good meal, that's for sure. Dang, look at those teeth!"

The muscular Teko warriors worked together to start pulling the creatures aboard. Suddenly, off in the distance, a large splash got their attention. They all froze and listened.

Bud turned around and looked at Little One with a worried look. "Uh-oh," Bud said.

Little One pointed to Bud's paddle. Suddenly, Bud saw a fast-moving, deep-blue spot of light on the surface of the lake off in the distance. It was quickly moving toward the canoes. "Tiga," Little One whispered.

A large tiga was closing in on them. As quickly as the Teko warriors looked up, they shifted their focus back to the trap containing egwa. The Teko were quick and focused with their motions.

Quickly now, they worked the trap, securing and pulling it aboard. The canoe rocked back and forth as the warriors grunted and strained, finally pulling the trap containing the flopping egwa aboard the canoe. The tiga was much closer now; the water churned more rapidly. Now, from twenty feet away, a blue wave of water moved quickly toward them, still picking up speed. Bud wondered why they weren't getting the canoe moving yet.

He was starting to worry. If the large tiga reached them as their canoe sat still in the water, they and their canoe would be torn into pieces by the razor-sharp mouth of the great tiga.

Bud looked back at Little One again with a very worried look. Time slowed down as the Teko moved with precision. "Little One?" Bud said nervously.

Little One again used hand signals to Bud, telling him to prepare to paddle.

Ten feet away, the tiga broke the surface and roared, its large, dark eyes suddenly glowing red as they fixed on the canoe as if the sharklike creature were a laser-guided missile. The Teko all started to paddle quickly. Bud joined in, firmly hanging onto his paddle.

The arms of the Teko moved quickly as they gripped their paddles with sheer determination. They were extremely fast. Front, back, front, back—the canoe moved forward with determination. Bud tried to keep up, but he flubbed a stroke and then got back into rhythm.

The Teko warriors remained focused and shifted their paddles, quickly turning the canoe back to the left and away from the giant tiga. Front, back, front, back—the canoe was moving fast again.

The tiga was no match for the speed and maneuvering skills of the Teko hunters. The tiga's large fins thrust forward, moving a large amount of water forward in a wave.

Then, just as suddenly as it had appeared, the tiga slowed down. Frustrated, the tiga kicked the surface hard with its mighty tail, its blue light changing to bright red as it dove deep into the lake in a single motion and disappeared.

"Yeah, baby!" Bud yelled out with delight as he turned around to smile at Little One.

Little One smiled back.

At last, with their canoe now quickly moving along the surface, the Teko hunting party was safe. The Teko appeared to relax now as they continued to paddle toward the safety of their home in the caves. It had been a very successful hunt, and Bud was proud of their catch.

The Teko warriors began to harmonize in loud, low-pitched notes and clicks. Bud could tell they were proud of the success of their hunt. Their beautiful songs, punctuated by rhythmic clicks, carried across the lake like violins and French horns to their homes deep within the caves, where their families eagerly awaited their safe return.

Bud tried to copy their singing as they all paddled in synchronized, smooth motions. Little One slapped Bud hard with his paddle on the shoulder and said, "Sssst."

Bud laughed. "Okay, okay, Little Dog Whisperer, I'll stop."

— 38 —

THE CELEBRATION BEGAN AS rhythmic sounds, and harmonized notes vibrated throughout the caves like a symphony. It reminded Bud of the Hawaiian choir he had heard when he was young.

Bud stood at the cave entrance. He listened in wonder at the harmonizing sounds echoing from the caves out across the lake. Bud climbed higher up on a small outcropping of rock above the cave entrance to get a better view. It was high enough to get a better perspective of the lake over many of the trees surrounding it.

"Incredible," remarked Bud as he looked around him. "I know," he muttered. "I'll take a video with my cell phone and make it sound like a National Geographic program."

He took out his cell phone and started recording the video, talking with a deep announcer voice as he panned the horizon: "An amazing light show far above. There is something surreal about it that appears to synchronize to the harmonies emanating from the caves. The glowing ice far above dances, glowing bright red and white, with streaks of blue and purple waving wildly and reflecting off the lake below. The light quickly grows and stretches as far as the eye can see. It is incredibly bright at times, illuminating the plant life growing around the lake with white, red, orange, and blue light. Yellow glowing lanterns float above the cave entrance in the air like Chinese sky lanterns. The lake biosphere is amazingly abundant with plant, animal, and lake life, each glowing in unique colors and patterns of light. The light fills every corner of the landscape. I guess you could say nature has a way of surviving where it should be pitch black. It is alive with light here at the lake."

Bud turned off the video camera on his phone. "Man, that sounded stupid."

Bud looked at his cell phone. "Why didn't I think of this earlier?" Bud said as he tried calling Sara. The phone beeped with the message "No Signal."

"Oh, well. It was worth a try." Bud started thinking more about the troubles at the camp above. He knew he needed to make some sort of plan to get back to the expedition camp.

Little One found Bud on top of the cave entrance and waved for him to follow him back into the cave.

When they arrived where Peter was recovering, Bud looked at Peter and smiled. Incredibly, Peter was standing upright and walking around.

"Hi, Bud!" Peter said casually, as if nothing were different.

"You look great!" Bud said.

"Yep, amazing, huh? Turns out the Teko are natural healers, and they have all sorts of amazing medicines and medical devices. And look—I can jump, too!" Peter jumped up and down with excitement and energy.

"Awesome! So you really feel good?" asked Bud.

"Yep. Oh, and they've been working on Casey, too. He acts even more like Tigger now! Wait until you see him. He had so much energy that he took off at a hundred miles an hour."

"I hope he's okay," Bud said.

"Don't worry, these Teko really are amazing."

"Cool. You'll never believe where I went," Bud said.

"Where?"

"I went on the lake and helped them catch the creatures we're gonna eat tonight—"

Just then, Little One joined the two of them and began clicking and making various sounds. By his hand gestures, it was clear it was time to go to the celebration, and they needed to go now.

The two boys followed Little One as Casey suddenly appeared and ran around them in circles a few times before falling into step with them.

"These Teko are way intelligent," Peter said. "Communication seems to be by combining whale-sounding songs, dolphinlike clicks, and a wide range of tones and notes."

"They're very cool. And best of all, they were able to cure your illness and turn Casey into a puppy again. They have amazing medicines."

Little One pointed to the three groups of Teko, who were gathering for the hunting celebration. Bud looked around the wide-open room, which had a very high ceiling that reminded him of a European cathedral. Large numbers of Teko gathered in three distinct areas within the room. Glowing rocks were placed in a large circle in the middle of the room. Teko warriors from each group wore what appeared to Bud to be the same hunting clothes that were worn in the canoes, along with headbands and necklaces made from leather, some sort of bead, and jewels. Using a long metal tool, three Teko moved the glowing rocks into the center of the room.

Little One pointed for the boys to take a seat. "Assigned seating, I guess?" Bud said as he snickered.

Bud noticed there were Teko who appeared to be miners that had brought the glowing rocks from other parts of the cave. He recognized the egwa caught on the hunt as they were placed on metal bars in the center of the room.

"Those are the fish we caught today, Peter," Bud said. "Cool, huh?"

"Very cool. They're huge," Peter said.

Bud realized the Teko used the glowing rocks to cook the food. They placed layers of grass and leaves around the egwa and then tied the fish together with dried vines. The Teko warriors then placed the metal bar on two metal stands, elevating the fish above the glowing rocks. Smoke and steam started rolling off the leaves when they were placed over the rocks. The steam and smoke collected in a column above and disappeared into the ceiling far overhead.

"Did you notice that diamonds are everywhere?" Bud asked Peter. "They even use diamonds for the tips of their weapons and basic tools. I also saw gold, iron, silver, and other metals all around the cave on my tour with Little One." Bud pointed at the Teko preparing the food. "Those are the Teko I hunted with in the canoe."

"Canoe?"

"I'll tell you later."

Bud noticed Teko with brightly painted faces that he assumed were males and females working together using glowing rocks in other parts of the room to cook food. It

213

wasn't long before they removed the fish from the metal bars and large leaves and collected the cooked egwa.

Little One helped a small, older-looking Teko, brightly dressed with long eyelashes, prepare the food for Peter and Bud. Bud thought she must be Little One's mother.

Little One placed a portion of the cooked fish on the surface of a wooden board along with other food that resembled small cooked potatoes. The egwa simmered as if they were on a fajita platter. Little One sprinkled what appeared to be seasoning on the fish from a wooden bowl. Bud thought his mother must have made the seasoning from the plants and mosses around the lake, as he could see dried leaves and small flowers in the bowl.

Peter tapped Bud on the shoulder and pointed to a cute beto with a glowing white body and eerie blue eyes that had landed near Little One, clearly focused on a free meal. "I wonder if it's going to poop on Little One, too?" Peter said.

Bud looked at the beto with a grin. Little One stroked its head, and it purred loudly, like a cat.

Bud watched as Little One gathered the hunters who had gone on the recent hunt. They began to sing a song that sounded and looked like a celebration reenacting the dangers of the recent hunting trip. The families circled around the singing hunters and began to dance.

Bud and Peter both watched in amazement as the group celebrated. An elderly looking Teko was very animated as he appeared to tell stories to Teko children who were seated around him, listening intently. The elder used gestures as he made clicks and tones that brought the stories to life.

A Teko leader placed a jeweled necklace around the neck of Little One, then placed one on Bud and motioned as if to congratulate them both for their successful hunt.

From outside the caves came a roar that caused the Teko to pause as it echoed through the caves, but only briefly. Little One turned to the elder with a worried, nervous look, but was quickly put at ease with a loving caress. The elder gestured that it was okay, and the celebration continued. Bud and Peter relaxed.

Bud whispered to Peter, "These Teko sure know their environment well and raise their children with love and security."

"Yeah, it seems like the Teko are completely part of the environment around them," remarked Peter.

A small group of Teko started to encourage Bud and Peter to join in the celebration. Bud and Peter laughed as they tried to mimic the Teko songs and dances.

The entire group danced and feasted as if there were no cares in the world, with Casey running in circles, jumping and barking.

As the time went on, Bud started thinking again about his father. Now that Peter was better, it was time to do something. He knew his father would be worried sick. Bud took a deep breath for the first time since they had arrived at the lake.

Bud turned to Peter, who had stopped dancing and was standing by Bud's side. "I'm worried about my dad and sister," Bud said. "I hope they're okay, with those goons bullying everyone around camp. I've been thinking about a plan. We need to get to the transport and try to contact my dad. Your wheelchair is there, and you can connect it to the communication backbone in the transport to talk with them from my cell phone and let him know we're okay."

"Sure thing—great idea," Peter said with a smile. "My dad is probably worried, too. Wait until he finds out that I can walk again!"

— 39 —

Bud approached Little One with a sense of urgency. "We need to get back to the transport," Bud said.

Little One looked into Bud's eyes. He made a series of clicks to the Teko around him, along with a series of quick hand gestures. Little One nodded.

A group of a dozen Teko gathered around them.

"Wow, that was quick," Bud said. One of the Teko motioned for Bud and Peter to follow them.

They quickly headed for the transport with Little One.

Once they arrived at the transport, Bud watched in amazement as ten of the Teko took positions around the transport, with two Teko watching in front of the transport doors. They looked as if they were patrolling the area.

"Sure is nice to have a Teko army as an escort," Peter said.

Bud quickly got to work on the outside of the transport. First he located the control box on the transport shaft and looked carefully at the schematic on the panel, then pulled a group of wires out and cut them with a tool he took from his backpack. He took out the wireless hub from his backpack and started the modifications to enable the transport communication system to talk with Peter's wheelchair computer.

"You didn't tell me you knew electronics, too," Peter said as he watched Bud with amazement.

"One of the benefits of working at the Space Center," Bud said as he twisted two wires together. "Larry showed me all sorts of cool things."

Suddenly the transport began to make noise. The doors shut, and the transport rumbled. It startled everyone.

"What did you do?" asked Peter.

"Huh? That's strange. Didn't do a thing. That wasn't me. Looks like the transport is back online again and headed back up to the camp," Bud said as he kept working on connecting his wireless network to Peter's wheelchair computer so he could use his cell phone. "Can you hold this for me?" asked Bud as he attached the antenna to the side of the transport.

Peter held the antenna and looked around at the Teko. "These Teko sure take things seriously. Where's Casey and Little One?"

"No clue. Little One is probably close by, and Case was playing like a puppy in the caves with those young Teko last I checked."

A few minutes later, the transport rumbled again. "Sounds like the transport is on its way back down here," Peter said.

"Jeez, that was quick," Bud said. "I'm almost finished."

"Hurry. That bully general may be on his way down here."

Two Teko felt the transport doors and put their heads against the metal structure, as if to listen. Moments later, the two inspecting Teko made a series of loud warning clicks, and the entire Teko group ran for the cover of the surrounding bushes and trees.

Little One appeared behind Peter and pushed him to get his attention. He motioned for them to go into the bushes.

Peter understood. "Let's hide. Quick!" Peter said. They ran for cover behind a large mulberry bush. The Teko prepared to throw their spears and blow the poison darts at whoever came out of the transport. Little One took a position next to Bud.

The transport doors opened.

Bud looked, but he couldn't see anyone in the transport. Then, unexpectedly, Sara's face peeked from behind the transport door.

"It's Sara!" Bud yelled as he ran out from behind the large bush. "It's okay, Little One—tell them it's okay."

After a series of clicks from Little One, the Teko relaxed and went back to patrolling the area around the transport.

"Bud! You're alive!" shouted Sara.

"Wow! OMG! This place is amazing," Tom said, stepping out of the transport behind Sara.

"What are you guys doing here?" asked Peter.

Both Sara and Tom looked at Peter with surprise. "Hey, how the ..." Tom said. "No way, Peter, you're walking. Peter, you're walking!" He ran up to Peter and hugged him.

Little One and two other Teko approached them.

Sara and Tom jumped when they first saw the Teko coming toward them. Sara grabbed at Tom's arm and screamed, "Tom!"

Tom was speechless.

"Don't worry, they're cool," Bud said as he hugged Sara.

"Yeah, pretty awesome, huh?" Peter pointed to the Teko around them. "These little guys fixed me up real good. They have some really cool medicines."

"How did you guys get down here?" asked Peter.

"Your dad was worried about you, so we created a little distraction and jumped into the transport when we noticed it was working again," Tom said, still staring at the Teko. "That darn transport keeps malfunctioning."

"Is Dad okay? What is that crazy bully general doing?" Bud said.

"They're so cute," Sara said as she studied them. Sara took a breath and focused back on Bud. "He's doing okay. Mainly worried about you, Bud. But the general shot Kurt."

"I know … we were there when it happened. Is he okay?"

"Yes, he's fine; it was just a flesh wound," Sara said. "That general is making ridiculous threats. He's taking over everything."

Bud looked at Peter. "That's what I was afraid of. We need to get this working, and really quick. I need to talk with my dad." Bud went back to working on his wireless communication connection.

Suddenly, a loud roar echoed near them. Sara screamed. Another loud roar erupted—this one closer still. The entire group of Teko disappeared except for Little One.

"Wh-where'd they go?" asked Tom.

"Don't worry, they'll keep us safe," Peter said as he helped Bud work on the transport.

Bud closed the panel door and then began work on opening the electrical panel. "Hey, maybe the Teko could help us take back the camp from the commandos," Bud said.

"How are they going to do that?" Tom asked. "The transport will only fit about … let's see, ten of them. Besides, the commandos have very large guns."

"*No problemo*," said Bud.

"Yeah," Peter said. "They have these small, pencil-like spears that they blow out of a wooden tube. The spears have some sort of poison on them that paralyzes their victims. And they move super fast. Their little legs seem to move as fast as the dolphins above move in the water. They glide through the air as they move."

Bud continued to try to open the electrical panel, but it was still stuck.

"They really do look like little dolphins with legs," Tom said.

"I'm really worried," Sara said. "Those commandos are ruthless. We need to do something!"

"Can you guys help me with this thing? I think it's stuck." Peter and Tom both grabbed part of the transporter electrical panel door. They both pulled, but it was not budging. They tried again. Suddenly it opened all at once, causing Peter and Tom to tumble down the ramp.

"Tom, Peter—are you guys okay?" asked Sara as she ran to Tom.

Tom jumped up and dusted off his pants. "Sure thing, Sara, I'm good. Sorry about that, Bud."

Peter stood up and flexed both his arms. "Check out these guns," he said.

Bud just rolled his eyes as he looked at Peter's skinny arms.

Bud studied the electrical drawing inside the panel they had just opened and worked quickly to add electrical power to his wireless communication device.

"There. That should do it," Bud said. He retrieved a cell phone from his backpack.

Peter, Tom, and Sara huddled around Bud as he held the cell phone. "Okay, all we need to do now is connect." Bud tapped on the screen of the cell phone. The speaker activated, and they could all hear the phone ring.

"But how is this going to work?" asked Sara. "They disconnected all communication to the outside world."

"We have a few special features we added to the communication system. We'll connect into the internal communications system and our webcams." Bud fiddled with the cell phone again. Finally it displayed the word "Connected," and a video image appeared.

"Genius. Absolute genius," Tom said, looking over Bud's shoulder.

"That's from our webcam," Peter said.

They could all see the control room and the commandos on the cell phone display. The team members remained in the corners of the room. Bud tapped a new set of numbers. Another image appeared, this time of the area around the transport clean room.

"What the heck?" Tom gasped.

"Just another additional feature, as we call them, that we added to the expedition camp," Bud said. He smiled at Peter.

"Way to go, little brothe—" Sara started when Bud interrupted.

"Sara, where's your cell phone?"

"Huh?"

"Your cell phone. You know, the one you grabbed in the computer room."

"Oh, yeah … ah … oh, I gave it to Dad," replied Sara. "He was going to try to get help."

"Excelente," Bud said as he tapped in a new number.

Bud's father's face suddenly appeared on the cell phone display.

"What … who … Bud? Is that you?" whispered Bud's father with a look of shock on his face.

"Dad, we're fine down here," Bud said. "We're with these dolphin people and—"

"Dolphin people? What?"

"Is it safe for you to talk?" asked Peter.

"Yes, for the moment. That crazy general is talking with his men about going down to the lake. Thank God you're all okay."

"Dad," Bud said. "We need to bypass the camp's communications. You need to dial *911 on the phone you're holding. Peter and I set up that phone to use a direct uplink we installed that bypasses the expedition camp's uplin—"

Bud's father interrupted again. "Direct uplink? You installed what?"

"Well, Peter and I made some, ah, modifications around the camp. You can yell at me later. Just dial *911 on the cell phone, and you will connect directly to Peter's father. He wanted to have direct access with Peter, so we used a parallel uplink and connected it to the communication satellite dedicated to the expedition."

"Okay, son. Got it. How do I call you back?"

"No need. We will be able to see and hear everything you do when you dial out. I will just set my phone into mirror mode."

"What mode?"

"Never mind—it is something Peter and I designed. It just means we will see and hear what you do when you call out on the phone you have there."

"Okay. Please be careful!" Tears welled up in his father's eyes.

Bud tapped the "Mirror" button. Bud looked at the transport as it started vibrating. The transport's doors closed unexpectedly and engaged.

"What did you do?" asked Peter.

"Not a thing. But we better hurry. Looks like the transport is on its way back to the camp again."

They could hear Bud's father entering *911 on the cell phone as each digit caused a tone sound. The message "Transmitting … Connected" appeared on Bud's phone.

Dr. Roberts answered the phone. "Peter?" asked Dr. Roberts, who sounded surprised on Bud's cell-phone speaker.

"No, Dr. Roberts, this is Dr. Thompson," Bud's father said.

"Is everything okay? Where is Peter?"

"Dr. Roberts, we have an emergency here," Bud's father said.

"Emergency?"

"Dad, I'm really, really good. Don't worry. But listen to Dr. Thompson. It's important—"

"Peter? What? Is that you?" asked Dr. Roberts. He sounded confused, and his voice trembled.

Bud's father interrupted. "Dr. Roberts, Peter is okay. Please ... we need your help," he whispered.

Bud could see commandos yelling at people in the other parts of the Mission Control room behind his father.

"Help? Sure, what's going on? Why is the communication link down?" Dr. Roberts said.

Bud's father spoke quickly. "Dr. Roberts, please listen carefully. General Jorge Hernandez and Argentine commandos have taken over the camp. Do you understand?"

"Oh, my. I, I, I—"

"Please, Dr. Roberts—we need you to focus. We need you to contact the central command authority deployed to Antarctica. Ask for Colonel Jerry Williams. He will know what to do. Can you do that?"

"Yes, yes, sure. I know Colonel Williams. Can I t-talk with Peter?" stammered Dr. Roberts.

"We don't have much time, Dr. Roberts. Just notify the authorities that we're in trouble here. I will call you again as soon as—"

Bud interrupted, "Dad, just tap the "Conference" button on your phone. It will add another line to our current call. Then hide your phone, and it will act like a relay, so we can talk to Dr. Roberts."

Bud's cell-phone display showed a commando in the background, walking around the perimeter of the room, inspecting each face carefully and getting closer to Bud's father.

"I have to go now," Bud's father whispered.

The phone display went black.

— 40 —

"Dr. Roberts, can you hear us?" asked Bud.

"Yes. You're still on the line?"

"Yes," Bud said, "my father must have had a chance to hit the button before the commando came over. Just press "Conference" on your phone to call Colonel Williams, and we'll help explain what's going on when he answers on the other end."

"Peter?"

"Dad, I'm fine. Please—we need to get help here quick."

They could hear Dr. Roberts touching the keypad to enter the phone number. "Central," the operator answered.

"This is Dr. Roberts. Please patch me through to Colonel Williams ASAP. There is an emergency situation at the expedition camp."

Bud, Peter, Tom, and Sara all huddled closer around Bud's cell phone to listen in using the speaker, since there was no video connection. The Teko continued to patrol the area around them, occasionally looking at what they were doing with curiosity.

"Right away, sir."

There was a beep, and then the phone connected. "Williams here."

"Colonel Williams, this is Dr. Roberts at UC Berkeley. We met at the last full session of the—"

Colonel Williams interrupted. "I am aware, Doctor. Thank you. What can I do for—"

Bud interrupted, "Sir, this is Bud Thompson. I am Dr. Thompson's son."

"You're at Berkeley?" replied Colonel Williams.

"No, sir, we're at the expedition, and—"

Colonel Williams interrupted, "We?"

"Ah, yes, sir. I am calling with my sister and Dr. Roberts's son, Peter, and Tom—"

"All right, so what the Sam Hill is going on, Mr. Thompson?" demanded Colonel Williams.

"It is a long story, but the Argentine general invaded the camp."

"Invaded the camp? How many men?"

"Well, not exactly sure, but a bunch."

"Now, Mr. Thompson, listen carefully," Colonel Williams said in a very calm, cool, and collected manner. "I need a more exact estimate. What sort of weapons? How many casualties?"

Bud looked at Peter and let out a sigh; all he remembered seeing was a lot of guys with guns.

Peter whispered, "I'd say about twenty and—"

"Just tell him," Bud said.

"Excuse me?" said Colonel Williams.

"Oh, sorry. Here is Peter Roberts."

Peter moved closer to the cell phone. "I would estimate at least twenty commandos wearing full attack gear, with

Russian issued AK-47s. One team member down with minor wounds."

Bud looked at Peter in surprise. "Since when do you know so much about the military?"

"My favorite movie is *Transformers*. Watched it at least a hundred—"

"Boys, please, we can hear you," said Dr. Roberts over the phone.

"Sorry, Dad," Peter said.

Just then, a very loud roar, along with a bellowing scream, echoed all around them. The Teko hunting party began to sing, harmonizing in what sounded like a symphony of violins and French horns.

"What the heck is that?" asked Colonel Williams.

"Well, sir. We're at the lake and—" started Bud.

Colonel Williams interrupted in a deep baritone voice, "You are where, Mr. Thompson?"

"We're at the lake with the Teko."

"The who?"

"Well, sir, the creatures that live here," Bud said.

"Damn it! Julie!" the Colonel barked, "Get me the president now!"

Bud continued, "We need to hang up, sir."

"Now wait just one —" started Colonel Williams.

Bud just said, "Just send help—and fast, sir," before he disconnected the line.

"Why'd you need to hang up?" asked Peter.

"Not much else to tell him at the moment. Besides, I figure he knows what to do."

They all sat still for a moment and looked at each other. A small group of Teko carried off another evil-looking creature close by.

"Now what?" asked Peter.

Sara, Tom, and Peter looked at Bud for an answer.
"We wait," Bud said.

$$- \; 41 \; -$$

WHILE THEY WAITED ON the transport ramp for the rest of the Teko group to return, Bud decided to scan through the webcams they had positioned throughout the expedition camp. He watched the general on his cell phone display and listened. The general barked out commands and pushed team members around like an overgrown bully as they tried to get the transport to work again. Bud switched from webcam to webcam, monitoring the general and listening to the audio. He was quite proud of his recent addition, which allowed him to hear whoever was around the webcam they installed. Peter agreed with him that it was a cool new "feature."

Bud looked up to see Tom holding Sara closely and comforting her. Bud smiled and shook his head—at last, a change from her constant complaining.

Peter worked on communications with Little One, trying to make similar sounds and use sign language. Little One was repeating and combining the clicking sounds of their language with hand signs to help Peter understand what he was saying.

Bud selected a new webcam, and he was shocked to see Kurt talking casually with the general. He tapped "Record" on his cell phone and zoomed in.

"It is good that you are bad shot, General," Kurt said.

"No, you are wrong, my Russian friend," said the general. "You're lucky I am such a *good* shot."

"You must get your men down to the lake immediately and collect as many diamonds as dey can carry. I am afraid not much time remains," Kurt said, rubbing his sore arm.

"You told me we had days to collect all we wanted from the lake. What has changed?" barked the General.

"An unplanned incident, as you know. You must take care of the group of four now down at lake. Your men must appear to attempt rescue. An unfortunate rescue gone badly," Kurt said as he smiled and shook his head. "The creatures below, of course, were just too much for you and … well, you know what to do." Kurt paused and then continued, "You will show world that lake is dangerous and must be controlled by military force. The Argentinean military force."

The general smiled, inhaling on his freshly lit cigar then blowing the smoke out as he talked. "Yes, I will be a hero. A rich hero!" He blew out the remaining smoke into the biggest smoke ring Bud had ever seen. It floated toward the ceiling as the general laughed uncontrollably in his deep baritone laugh.

"You must collect as many diamonds as possible, as we will not have another chance to communicate while you remain here. I will expect my cut to be deposited as usual," said Kurt, who looked nervous now. "I must return now."

"Of course, of course," the general said as he continued to laugh. "Jose will take care of this, as he always does." Kurt left the hallway as the general laughed harder.

Bud yelled, "Guys, over here, quick! Kurt is in on the camp takeover. I've been monitoring our webcams and just heard Kurt talking to the general. They're planning to kill us and make it look like the Teko did it." Bud added in a panicked voice, "We need a new plan, and quick. They'll be here soon!"

"What about getting Little One to help us?" Tom asked.

"Good idea. We don't have much time. Peter, can you try and communicate with Little One that we need his help? We will need the help of his best hunters."

After a brief discussion, Little One disappeared.

A short time later, he returned with a group of Teko.

"Let's go now," Bud said. "Everything seems to be working with my cell phone connection. We should be able to connect from the caves using wifi now and monitor the video from there and see anyone who uses the transport."

"Cool," Peter said. "Let me tell Little One."

Little One understood and motioned for them to follow. He took off quickly, making a loud, high pitched clicking sound that rang in Bud's ears.

"Where are we going now?" asked Sara, who was holding tightly onto Tom.

"To their caves. I'm betting it is much safer than staying here."

"Caves?" asked Sara.

"Yeah, wait until you see them," Bud said.

"Hey, where's Casey?" asked Sara, looking around.

"He's back at the caves we're talking about," Peter said.

"Yeah, playing with a bunch of young Teko," Bud said. "Wait 'til you see him. He acts like a little puppy again."

The entire group headed quickly toward the Teko caves, with Little One leading the way.

— 42 —

As Bud walked back to the Teko caves behind Peter and Little One, he continued to watch and listen to the webcam near the transport up at the expedition camp using his cell phone; the connection was working nicely.

The Argentinean general was pacing back and forth, puffing on his long Cuban cigar and smiling. "It will not be long now. I will have diamonds."

"Of course! Peter," Bud yelled, "he's after the diamonds. That's what the general really wants." Bud kept watching and walking at the same time.

Peter just walked in stride with Little One, who looked very serious and seemed in a hurry to get back to the caves.

Bud watched a commando guard position himself at the transport up above at camp.

"General, my general," called out the commando to the soldiers around him. "The transport is working again. It has returned." A small group of commandos ran over to the transport clean room and stood close to the transport door with their guns ready.

Bud watched as the transport doors opened. The guards lunged forward toward the opening transport doors with their weapons aimed. Nothing. It was empty.

Bud laughed as he watched. "Now that wouldn't have been very smart for us to do, now would it."

"General, General, the transport has returned empty," a commando said.

Bud continued watching.

The general ran over to the transport and did his own inspection. "Very good. You five men prepare to come with me to the lake. Bring my gear." The general spoke loudly and deeply, so he would be overheard by the expedition team members who were being held close by. "We will rescue the unfortunate young people who have become trapped down at the lake."

Bud stopped in the cave and just stood there, watching the video.

The general moved quickly with a large empty bag over his shoulder. Five fully armed commandos followed him into the transport. The general engaged the transport, and the doors closed with a sudden jerk.

Bud watched as the transport made its way downward to the lake.

"Guys, we need to hurry," Bud said. "The general is on his way now."

Bud switched the webcam to the one he had just installed. Nothing—the video was just static.

"Dang, it was working before. Why isn't it working? Let me try—" Bud concentrated as he tapped frantically on the cell phone. Finally, a video appeared. The door was still closed, "Whew, good—they're not here yet," Bud said to himself.

Peter and Little One had disappeared once they arrived at the caves. Bud figured they were getting the Teko hunting party prepared.

He sat down with Tom and Sara in the cave, huddling closely so they could all watch the video on the cell phone that showed the transport.

After a short time, the transport doors opened.

Bud jumped. "They're here now," Bud said. He looked around for Peter.

Bud looked back down to the video. A group of heavily armed commandos lunged outward, weapons moving quickly from side to side.

"Clear, clear, clear," they called. "All clear, my general."

The general walked slowly out of the transport behind them. "We must quickly eliminate the four unplanned distractions," the general said.

"I'm scared. Those crazy men want to kill us!" Sara said as she held onto Tom's arm tightly.

They all kept watching the video.

The general smiled as he looked back and forth, surveying the diamonds on the ground, which could be seen everywhere in all shapes, sizes, and colors.

"Magnificent." He picked up a large diamond and looked closely at it before stuffing it in his empty bag.

"He's collecting the diamonds," Bud said. "I can't believe that."

"I bet each diamond is worth hundreds of thousands of dollars on the open market," Tom said.

"General, over here. They went this way," one of the commandos said as he crouched on one knee, inspecting the tracks left by four pair of shoes and an oddly shaped foot in the mud.

"They saw our tracks," Tom said, his voice trembling.

The men moved forward in front of the general, crouched down, and moved slowly, carefully scanning from left to right, right to left.

Off in the distance came a loud roar. The men stopped and looked at the general with fear.

"Move onward, cowards. We must find them quickly," the general yelled, blowing out a large puff of cigar smoke.

The men turned and moved faster.

The general blew out another puff of smoke. His eyes refocused on the diamonds all around him. He smiled as he continued filling his bag as they walked.

In the cave, Peter walked over to the three of them. "The Teko are ready. Let's go with them. We can watch about one hundred feet from the cave entrance," Peter said. "They will ambush them on the trail."

"Cool," Bud said. "Let's go kick that bully's big butt."

— 43 —

LITTLE ONE GRABBED a large horn and blew. It bellowed as he sounded the Teko alarm. In seconds, a group of two dozen Teko, fully armed, had assembled around them and were ready for battle.

Bud thought they acted like firemen back home responding to a fire alarm. Just like firemen, they didn't know the exact danger; they just knew there was danger.

The Teko moved out quickly toward the general and his men. More Teko appeared, and then still more. The Teko were obviously taking this threat seriously.

"Holy cow! I had no idea there were so many of them," Bud said to Peter.

The Teko took positions in the trees, on outcroppings, and in the shadows along the path. The Teko were everywhere, their camouflage blending nicely into the vegetation. Each Teko had a set of weapons ready.

Bud could hear the commandos moving through the vegetation as the general barked, "Move! Hurry!"

The Teko had not yet made their presence known and were now completely surrounding the general and his commando team.

Sara and Tom stood behind Bud and Peter. They were all positioned behind a large, glowing, burr-covered bush the size of Bud's old oak tree.

Sara heard a noise behind her. She whirled around, her eyes wide. A beto was stretching its wings. Sara screamed; they all jumped.

"Shhh!" whispered Bud loudly. Tom looked at Bud, rolled his eyes, and then put his arms around Sara to comfort her.

Sara looked softly at Tom and whispered, "Sorry."

Bud could see commandos had heard Sara's scream and were now in full alert mode as they looked around. The general grabbed a machine gun from one of the commandos and ran forward.

"Come out, you American pigs!" the General pulled the trigger and held it. A long burst of bullets flew in the direction of Sara's scream.

The Teko unloaded on the commandos. Bud had never seen so many arrows, spears, and other flying weapons raining down at one time. The Teko weapons struck the commandos like a cloud of hungry mosquitoes. The Teko weapons were not meant to kill; the tips of the darts had a toxin that would render the men paralyzed until they were given the antidote. Bud knew from experience how that worked.

All of the commandos were hit as the darts landed on their targets. The general dropped to his knees. The gunfire stopped as suddenly as it had begun.

Bud and Peter ran to the scene now that it was over.

Bud looked around. Three Teko had been struck by the random bullets fired by the general's gun. They were quickly tended to by other Teko near them and taken back to the caves. It had taken only seconds for this entire scene to unfold.

Bud turned to see Peter crying, crouched over Little One.

"Peter! Peter! What's wrong?" Bud yelled as Tom, Sara, and Bud all ran to where Peter was with Little One.

Peter continued crying. "Little One! A bullet hit him, Bud. He's not moving. I think he's dead." Little One lay still—too still. He was not breathing.

Two Teko ran to them and started aggressively working on Little One. Little One remained lifeless; he didn't move, and Bud didn't see him breathing. They all watched in horror as two Teko quickly carried Little One off toward the caves.

Other Teko secured the incapacitated commandos. The general was struggling, but to no avail; he, too, had been hit with one of the poison-tipped darts. He was still able to speak as he was being carried off. He yelled, continuing to rattle out commands.

"Kill them! You fools, get up, you cowards! Get them!" But none of the other commandos could move.

The general squirmed as he worked to try to free himself, but he only managed to move slightly in small, jerky motions.

The Teko quickly moved the general and the group of commandos into the caves.

— 44 —

Bud sat in the Teko cave, watching the webcams up at the expedition camp on his cell phone display. Colonel Williams had arrived from his temporary base thirty miles away. He paced in the makeshift command center at the camp entrance building. Peter had convinced Bud to place a webcam in the entrance building in order to see who was coming and going. As it turned out, Peter's idea had been a good one.

Bud scanned the webcams showing Colonel Williams's men positioned along two of the walls close to the entrance into the expedition-camp tents. Bud watched a commando walk near the entrance. Colonel Williams's men quickly secured and removed the commando. Bud was impressed.

Bud tried to contact his father, but for some reason, he could not connect to the cell phone Sara had given to their father. Then Bud tapped a few times on his cell phone, switched to the webcam nearest Colonel Williams, and listened.

"I'm getting tired of this cat-and-mouse game," said Colonel Williams to one of his men. "We have the element of surprise here, and all we're allowed to do is sit and wait outside of the expedition camp? I've had enough of this waiting for approval from the president."

Bud looked at the display and let out a frustrated sigh. He couldn't communicate with the colonel. He watched Colonel Williams pace, growing more restless and impatient.

"Enough of this," the colonel said. "I am done waiting. I suppose it is better to ask the president for forgiveness than permission." The colonel looked determined. He keyed his radio. "Sergeant, I want five men at each exit in two minutes. We're taking this damn camp and taking it now!"

"They're going to retake the camp," shouted Bud. Everyone huddled around Bud's cell phone to watch.

"Alpha One, Alpha Two, Alpha Three … engage and secure," the sergeant spoke in a confident monotone, as if he did this every day. "On my go."

"Three … two … one … go, go, go!" The sergeant's tone changed from a monotone to a higher pitched, excited tone. The team quickly entered each entrance.

Bud tapped on his display to switch between webcams to follow the action.

The commandos were caught off guard. Machine-gun fire rattled in short bursts as commandos attempted to fight back. As they watched on the cell phone video, Colonel Williams's team secured the hallways easily as the commandos quickly surrendered to Colonel Williams's men.

Bud tapped the cell phone again and saw his father trying to use the modified cell phone in the Mission Control room. He was frantically tapping on the phone, trying to reconnect to Bud without success, when the American Special Forces team showed up.

Bud watched as, one by one, the commandos were captured by Colonel Williams's team with amazing speed. One commando saw them coming and shot a burst of bullets. The team responded with three bullets fired in a short burst that instantly disabled the commando. The remaining commandos threw down their weapons, put their hands behind their heads, and dropped to their knees.

"Wow, our guys are good," Bud said. "Did you see how fast they captured those commandos?" Bud frantically tapped on the cell phone and switched to the webcam near his father. "Thank goodness Dad is okay. But I still can't connect to his phone."

Peter watched the cell phone video sadly with a distant look in his eyes. "I'm glad your dad is okay," he said softly as he walked away with his head down.

Bud watched as Colonel Williams walked casually into the room. "Dr. Thompson?"

"Yes, yes, over here, Colonel."

"Good. Glad you're safe. Nice to see you again."

"Colonel, we must act quickly. My kids are down at the lake, and the general has a team of commandos down there."

Bud wanted to tell them that the commandos had been captured by the Teko already, but he still couldn't connect to the cell phone his father was holding; it just wasn't working.

"We need to get down there now," Bud's father said.

The colonel looked at Bud's father and then gave the sergeant who had led the team into the room an intense look; he didn't need to say a word. The sergeant didn't hesitate. He pressed the radio handset secured to his vest. "Alpha One, report."

"Colonel, this is Alpha One. Expedition camp is secure."

"Roger that, Alpha One. Report to my position on the double."

"Yes, sir. Alpha One en route. Out."

"They did it," Bud yelled. Everyone joined in the celebration—everyone except for Peter. "Where'd Peter go?" asked Bud, looking around.

— 45 —

BUD FOUND PETER ALONE in an empty part of the cave, crying.

"You okay?" asked Bud.

"How could they? Little One? Dead?" cried Peter. "They killed Little One."

"I know. It's not fair," Bud said.

Just then, the colorful butterfly Bud had seen before returned, fluttering gracefully around Peter's head, almost appearing to comfort him.

Peter smiled. "A butterfly. Look, Bud, it's beautiful."

Bud smiled back.

Peter's serious expression returned as he said, "I saw the picture, ya know."

"What picture?"

"You know, your picture. The one you carry with you."

"Oh, you mean this one?" Bud pulled the picture of him and his mother out of his pocket. He then said softly, "She gives me strength when I don't know what to do."

"How long has she been gone?" Peter asked.

"Over five years now," Bud said, looking closely at the picture. "But it feels like she is close." The butterfly circled around the picture and then back to Peter, floating around his head and tickling his forehead with its wings.

Peter smiled. "Butterflies are like that for me."

"What do you mean?" Bud carefully put the picture back in his pocket.

"Well, when I need the strength of my mother, I sometimes see a butterfly and it puts me at ease. Almost like she's here with me. Does that sound weird?"

"Not at all. That's cool."

Both boys watched the butterfly flutter off slowly.

"I often feel my mother is close by, too," Peter said quietly.

Bud took a deep breath and put his arm around Peter. "I'm sure she is," Bud reassured him. "C'mon, let's go."

They walked over to a small section of the cave where the general and his commandos were being held. Bud looked them over. Two Teko were standing guard with large, diamond-tipped metal spears.

The Teko had just given their captors the antidote in order to prevent permanent damage. Bud noticed the general was working on the knots that had been tied to hold his hands firmly behind his back, but Bud wasn't worried, since he knew the Teko were so darn good at tying knots.

One of the elder Teko approached Bud and the rest of the group. He made a number of gestures and clicks. Bud looked at him with a blank expression.

Peter looked closely at the elder Teko. "He says it's time to go back to our world and leave theirs."

"Dad will be worried," Sara agreed. "We should really go."

Tom helped Sara stand, although she really didn't need his help.

"Okay, we understand," Bud tried to tell the elder Teko, making some crazy hand motions. Sara looked at Bud and rolled her eyes.

A group of Teko helped the group of commandos to their feet, along with the arrogant general. The entire group started back to the transport.

The general started making demands. "Please, please—my bag, my bag. I must have my bag."

Tom grabbed the bag that was so important to the general. "What's in this thing? It's heavy," Tom said as he heaved it over his shoulder.

Bud walked over to Tom and opened the bag to take a look. "Diamonds. He's stealing diamonds from the Teko. I saw him on the webcam. Empty the diamonds out, and give him back his precious bag—but only after it's empty."

"Sure thing," Tom said. He emptied the bag while the general protested loudly.

A Teko warrior pushed Tom and gestured for him to follow.

"Guys, c'mon. They want us to get back to the transport," Tom yelled as he helped Sara navigate through the vegetation.

Just as they neared the transport, the general freed his hands from the rope. A small, jagged diamond fell to the ground as the general pushed Tom, grabbed his empty bag, and disappeared into the vegetation.

"Shouldn't we go after him?" Bud asked a Teko elder. The Teko elder appeared to understand, but just shook his head in disgust and made calming hand motions.

Bud immediately relaxed. They continued toward the transport.

When they arrived at the transport, Bud heard a loud splash in the distance. Everyone turned their heads, but it was Bud who ran to the far side of the ramp, looking out at the lake on his tiptoes. He saw the general bent over near the lake's edge, scooping up the glistening jewels, but he also noticed a fin in the water.

"Uh-oh," Bud said, watching as the tiga stalked his unsuspecting prey.

"Bud," Sara called out, "let's go!" She walked up alongside him, pulling on his arm, but then stopped to see what he was looking at.

"Go!" Bud shouted at her, not wanting her to see what was about to happen.

Sure enough, the tiga closed in like a torpedo locked on its target. Its large top dorsal fin, now fully exposed, glided smoothly and swiftly through the water toward the general.

The general looked up. Bud watched as the general froze, then suddenly realized what was happening. He turned and unsuccessfully attempted to move his feet, which had sunk down in the soft mud.

Too late.

The tiga quickly closed in. The massive tiga launched itself into the shallow waters and onto the muddy shoreline. It moved its body with determination as it moved back and forth in the mud. The tiga greeted the general with its large, wide open jaws and dagger-sized teeth. Splash, whoop—the tiga kicked its caudal fin back and forth, hard.

The general screamed again, but this time it was muffled.

The tiga kicked hard and now moved away from the shoreline and back into the depths of the lake with the general firmly held in its jaw. Then the lake fell silent as the tiga pulled the general under the water.

Sara screamed and turned away.

The water turned bright red; the general was gone. Small bubbles rose to the surface of the lake as the tiga's top dorsal fin slowly sank into the depths of the dark lake.

Bud looked away, grabbing Sara's arm so she would follow him to the front of the transport. He looked at the Teko elder, who gave a forced half smile that faded into a look of sorrow. Bud looked down, shaking his head.

Bud decided to try again and dialed the cell phone his father had with him. Suddenly, his father appeared onscreen. "Bud?"

"Dad! You finally got the phone working again! Cool!"

"Yes, one of the team members helped me with it. I have good news, too—the commandos have been captured up here. We're ready to come down to the lake with Colonel Williams's men."

"Hold tight—we're on our way up to the camp," Bud said, "We'll explain when we get there. Just let Colonel Williams know we have some prisoners for him."

"Prisoners?"

"Yep, gotta go. Be right up," Bud said as he disconnected the cell phone and got into the transport.

The Teko placed the tied-up men into the transport. The Teko handed Bud, Tom, and Sara spears with sparkling diamond tips as they packed into the transport with the tied-up commandos. Peter was the last to enter.

They all waved good-bye to the Teko standing on the transport ramp.

Just as the transport doors were about to shut, Bud remembered. "Oh, no—where is Casey?" Bud asked in a panic, looking around frantically.

As if on cue, Casey exploded from the bushes and plowed into the transport. The general's bag of diamonds hung from his mouth by its strap.

"Casey, every time I see you, you have more energy and you look younger!" Bud hugged Casey, took the bag, and handed it to the Teko elder. "These are yours," Bud said.

Sara smiled as Tom put both arms securely around her waist.

Peter looked sadly at the control panel and softly pressed the transport's "Engage" button. Bud patted him on his back, trying to comfort him.

The doors closed. Up they went until they arrived at the expedition camp.

The transport doors opened.

"Thank God," Bud's father said with a look of relief on his face. Before Bud's father could move, Sara ran toward him, embraced him, and said, "Dad, Dad! I love you! I love you so much!" Sara began to sob. They held each other tightly.

"It's been a long time since I saw them hug each other like that," Bud said to Peter. "Guess it was overdue."

Peter gave Bud a half smile and looked down, walking sadly out of the elevator.

— 46 —

Bud stood by as his father showed Colonel Williams the video Bud had captured on his phone of Kurt conspiring with the general. Bud was proud that his father wanted to handle Kurt all by himself, but Bud insisted that he be with his father when Kurt was confronted. That way, Bud could show the video if Kurt tried to deny it. Colonel Williams agreed reluctantly to stand by with his men, ready in case there were complications.

Bud and his father approached Kurt at the control-room console where Kurt sat working on one of the systems that had malfunctioned.

Bud's father gave Kurt a heavy tap on his shoulder.

"Ah, comrade, you startled me," Kurt said as he looked over his shoulder at them.

Kurt took a breath and appeared to relax. "Dr. Thompson. Congratulations on the return of your family. I am relieved they're safe. Hello, Mr. Bud. It is nice to see you safe."

Bud's father's face turned red. "Really? Really, Kurt? How could you?" His nerves were obviously starting to get the best of him.

Bud's heart was pounding. He couldn't remember his father ever being so angry.

"Excuse please? What do you mean?" Kurt said in a completely innocent voice.

"We have a video of you and the general."

Kurt held his arm and replied, "*Da*, my arm is still in pain, yes?"

"You lied to me. You betrayed me, betrayed the expedition. You endangered my family! Why? Why would you do such a thing?"

Kurt got up slowly and stood directly in front of Bud's father with a very calm look on his face. Then, without warning, Kurt shoved him using one hand with full force, launching Bud's father backward and onto his back. He fell hard onto the floor.

Kurt grabbed his lab coat and ran quickly out of the room before Bud could even move.

Finally Bud reacted, moving quickly to the control panel. He turned on the switch of the control-panel intercom. "He's running, he's running. Colonel Williams, he is running! My dad's hurt!" Bud shouted into the microphone, broadcasting his voice across the entire expedition camp.

Colonel Williams responded on his radio, "Medic, medic—get a medic in the Mission Control room. Dr. Thompson is hurt. Alpha One, Two, Three. Secure Dr. Popov. The Russian will be at one of your positions in thirty seconds. Just stay calm, Bud. Help is on its way," the Colonel said in a calm and reassuring, but firm voice.

Bud felt responsible. "Dad, you okay?"

"Yes, yes, I'm fine. Colonel Williams will take care of Kurt," Bud's father said as the medics arrived.

"Dad, I need to go after him." Bud knew his father would be taken care of now since the medics had arrived. Now Bud was angry. He decided he would be the one to get the traitor—who was also a bully in Bud's mind.

Before his father could argue with him, Bud took off out the door of the Mission Control room. He looked down the hallway in both directions and didn't see Kurt. Bud took out his cell phone and activated his helicopter and the Swarm, which were in the computer room.

Peter was talking with his father when Bud called.

"Hello?" Peter said.

"Peter, open the computer room door, and quick."

"Bud? What? Why?"

"No time to explain." Bud disconnected and started scanning the webcams on his cell phone. Finally he located Kurt. He activated the helicopter's autolocation mode and dialed in the location where he wanted the helicopter to go, since it could get there faster than he could. He quickly tapped his cell phone a few more times and configured the Swarm to follow the helicopter.

Bud located Kurt on a webcam and watched Kurt on his cell phone, running toward the expedition back entrance. Bud picked up the pace and started running at full speed while watching the video on his cell phone.

Kurt was gripping his lab coat tightly in one hand as he ran with his other in a sling, which made him run strangely. "Got something in your coat pocket, do you?" mumbled Bud as he ran down the hallway, watching the video.

Casey barked from behind Bud and moved faster, catching up.

The helicopter arrived first, with the dragonflies of the Swarm closely behind. They came to a stop and hovered where Bud had guessed Kurt might go. Bud switched to the helicopter webcam. Sure enough, there was Kurt. He had slowed down and put his lab coat on one arm and draped it over his other shoulder. He appeared startled by the hovering helicopter and the Swarm.

Kurt kept walking arrogantly, with a smile.

Bud zoomed in. "So you have a grin on your face, do you?" Bud slowed down, jogging toward the back entrance as he took control of the helicopter.

Kurt pushed the door open and ran through the door into the temperature-controlled area where Casey had relieved himself when Bud's family had first arrived at camp. Bud's helicopter stayed with Kurt, hovering over his head.

"Freeze! Hands behind your head and on your knees! Now!" yelled the Alpha One team leader. Kurt fell to his knees and put his free hand behind his head.

Casey ran ahead of Bud, pushing through the doors so hard that they locked in the open position. The dog jumped on Kurt's back at full speed, and Kurt slammed facedown to the ground.

Growling loud and deep, Casey stood proudly on Kurt's back, biting the man's collar and shaking it passionately back and forth.

"Way to take the bad guy down, Casey!" Bud said, grinning from ear to ear.

Kurt grimaced. "Get off, you—" Kurt yelled as he looked up to see a gun pointed two inches from his face. It was Colonel Williams, standing large and in charge.

The Alpha team completely surrounded Kurt, providing backup for Colonel Williams.

"Thought you might want to run, Dr. Popov," Colonel Williams said calmly. "Looks like the puppy likes you."

Colonel Williams and his team laughed as Bud grabbed Kurt by the shoulder with one hand, securing Casey with his other.

Kurt groaned. Suddenly, Kurt moved in close to Bud, his mouth positioned next to Bud's ear.

"Freeze!" yelled the Alpha One team leader.

Kurt had just enough time to whisper in Bud's ear, so only Bud could hear him.

"It is too bad about your mother's accident," Kurt said with an evil grin and then turned away, laughing.

Bud was shocked. "What? What did you say?" He shook Kurt. "What did you say about my mother?"

"Easy, big guy. We have him now, Mr. Thompson," said the colonel. He gave Bud's shoulder a tap of reassurance. The Colonel's men secured Kurt, and Bud backed away, still in shock.

Bud remembered Kurt's lab pockets were bulging and pointed it out to Colonel Williams.

"Whatchya got in them there pockets, Dr. Popov, that is so important to you?" asked Colonel Williams.

Kurt gave Bud a deathly stare, grinned, and then looked away.

The colonel looked at the Alpha One team leader and signaled with his head to open Kurt's pockets. The commander opened one pocket, and diamonds fell to the ground.

Bud's father arrived just in time to see the diamonds fall. "The samples? You took the diamond samples from the explorers? What a fool I've been," Bud's father said in disgust.

"Take this scum out of here," said Colonel Williams. "His Russian colleagues will have to deal with him now.

I hope you like Siberia; I hear the prison this time of year is nice and cold."

"Thank you, Colonel," Bud's father said with a sigh.

"Good work, Bud," said Colonel Williams. "I'm thinking your dog deserves a medal for that takedown."

Bud was still distracted by what Kurt had whispered to him. "Yes, sir, thank you," Bud muttered.

Bud's father looked at Bud and smiled. "Good work, son."

Bud nodded with some swagger and then commanded his heli and Swarm to hover in formation directly in front of him. He tapped twice on his cell phone, engaging the heli and Swarm to move forward. Bud followed them back slowly in the direction of the computer room to meet Peter with Casey walking by his side.

He pulled out the picture of his mother and took a long look.

"Thanks, Mom," Bud said with a smile, still wondering about what Kurt had whispered in his ear.

— 47 —

Bud sat in the cafeteria alone, using his fork to move his mac and cheese in circles on his plate. He couldn't get Kurt's comment out of his head. He tried to ignore it, but Kurt's evil grin rattled him. *What happened to my mom?* He wondered. It had been over five years now, and he couldn't remember any details. Actually, he tried hard never to think about it, and no one in the family ever talked about it.

Suddenly, a tray made a loud thud, appearing on the table right next to him. "How you doing, son?" asked Bud's father.

"Oh, uh, good. Thanks, Dad." Bud looked at his father with a half grin and then back down at his mac and cheese, continuing to move it in circles.

"Are you sure? You've seemed … well, distant since we caught Kurt," his father said with a concerned look on his face.

"I'm okay. I guess Kurt just surprised me, that's all. I mean, why would he—"

"I know. He surprised all of us," interrupted his father.

"He said something, too. Something I don't understand," Bud said now, looking at his father, his eyes filling with tears. "Actually, it was more how he said it than what he said."

"What? What did he say to you?" his father said. He put his arm around Bud's shoulders to comfort him.

"He said it was too bad about Mom. Did he know Mom?"

"Why, no. Well, I don't think so. The first time I met Kurt was when we arrived at the expedition camp," he said. "Maybe he was just trying to get back at you for catching him. He was probably trying to shake you up."

"How did Mom die? I mean, I don't remember any details about it."

His father looked around. Bud thought he seemed to be trying to muster up the words. He cleared his throat. "She was on a research trip to Moscow and—" He stopped as if he had just realized something and then continued. "She was doing some testing at Lomonosov, Moscow State University. On her way back to her hotel, she was in a car accident." His voice started to crack with emotion.

"Isn't that the same university that Kurt was at?" Bud asked.

"Ah." His father made a face. "Yes, I just realized that, too."

"What research was she doing?" asked Bud.

"She was working on biochemistry and the early stages of a genetic engineering project. The State Department asked her to review one of the science projects in Moscow."

"Do you know what the project was?" Bud asked.

"No, they would never tell me, and … well, I had you and your sister to tend to. That's when Grams came to stay with us and help me," he said. A tear ran down his cheek. "I'm sure it's just a coincidence that he taught at the same university."

There wasn't any more to say. Bud just had more questions that didn't have answers. "I miss her," Bud muttered, wiping his eyes and then his runny nose with his napkin.

"Me, too, Bud. Me, too."

— 48 —

Two weeks later, Bud walked with Sara and their father toward the expedition camp transport. "So what's going to happen to Kurt and those commando bullies?" asked Bud.

"Well, the UN Council sanctioned the Argentine government and placed General Hernandez's remaining officers under arrest. Argentina's president has apologized and has offered support." Bud's father continued, "Security is going to be tightened, and access to and from the lake will be strictly enforced, so you can't just go down whenever you want. All the nations have agreed that no one country will be in charge, and the Teko will be established as an independent nation. For now, we're calling it the Nation of Teko."

"That's cool," Bud said.

"Oh, and a new elevator transport is to be installed to further allow access to and from the lake, while providing a backup to the original transport, which seems to malfunction regularly."

Sara smiled. "Good thing!"

"Scientists like Peter's father are still sorting out the Teko language, but sign language is helping to aid in communication," Bud's father said. "I will lead the talks with the Teko elders. The Teko have also agreed to escort teams of explorers around the area and demonstrate their hunting techniques. We're approved to take limited samples and to observe how this lake ecosystem evolved. Scientists are now thinking the lake ecosystem and its creatures evolved over hundreds of thousands of years, separate from humans."

"I'm getting comments now from all my friends on Facebook," Sara said with an ear-to-ear satisfied grin. "It seems everyone wants to know about the daily discoveries at the lake. I never thought I would be so popular."

"Thanks for getting me permission to go down to the lake with Peter," Bud said to his father. "Peter's been pretty bummed out lately. It was like pulling teeth to get him to help me explore the caves to interpret those drawings we found on the cave walls."

"I know it's been hard on Peter," his father said sadly. "As time allows, I will assign more scientists to help you interpret those drawings. But we will be keeping those drawings under wraps for now. Colonel Williams said the drawings are officially classified as Top Secret for the time being. That means no mentioning them on Facebook, Sara, or tweeting about them, Bud."

They both nodded.

"What assignment did they give you, Sara?" asked Bud.

"I'll be helping teach the Teko about the many cultures that exist in the world above them. I'm really excited about it," said Sara, who hadn't complained at all since she had returned from the lake. "Tom's coming with us, too," Sara added, blushing.

They arrived at the transport and looked around for Tom and Peter.

"Here they come," Bud said.

Tom gave Sara a long hug. Bud pinched Sara.

"Ouch. Stop it, little brat!" Sara said with a grin on her face.

"Hey, Peter," Bud said.

"Hi. Thanks for inviting me," Peter said reluctantly. Bud could tell he was still down in the dumps.

They all squeezed into the elevator transport. Bud pressed the activation button, and the doors started to shut; Casey jumped in late, as usual.

"Should have known you wanted to come, too, Case," Bud said with a chuckle.

"Let's all be careful while we're at the lake, okay?" Bud's father said in a caring, fatherly voice as the elevator took them all downward. "Check in with me in the main cave often, okay?"

"Sure, but we'll be fine," Bud said. "The Teko elders will guide us around."

Down they went to the lake. The transport slowed and then stopped as it let out a burst of air. The doors of the transport shaft opened with a clunk.

Standing right in front of the entrance to the transport was Little One with a big smile on top of his natural smile. The same beautiful butterfly circled gracefully above Little One's head.

"Little One!" Bud and Peter shouted at the same time.

"You're alive! Oh, you're alive," Peter said as he started to tear up. He ran over to Little One and gave him a big hug.

Bud noticed Little One had tears swelling up in his large eyes. Bud ran over to him and hugged him alongside of Peter.

"You're okay, you're okay!" Peter kept saying.

"I'm so happy you're okay!" Bud said.

Little One clicked and sang as he hugged both boys.

Sara began to cry as she watched the reunion. "This is so cute," Sara said. She looked at Tom, who came over to her and held her close. They kissed. Bud saw it out of the corner of his eye and smiled. It was nice seeing her happy at last.

"Now, now, young lady, we had better get going," Bud's father said with a grin on his face as he watched Tom and Sara in their romantic embrace.

"Okay, Daddy," Sara said with a big smile.

"Mustn't keep the Teko waiting. Let's go, kids," Bud's father said.

Bud couldn't stop smiling. He was happy that Little One was okay and even happier that Peter was smiling again.

Off they all went to teach, learn about, discover, and explore this new underground world, their new friends the Teko, and the amazing creatures of the lake.

— Epilogue —

Bud sat at his father's desk in the expedition camp with his feet up on the table and a computer keyboard in his lap. Bud was studying images of the human drawings found in the Teko caves on his father's computer while everyone else was down at the lake.

The phone rang.

"Hello?"

"Dr. Thompson?" asked the lead scientist.

Bud took his feet off his father's desk and sat up straight in his chair. "No, sir, this is Bud Thompson. My dad is working at the lake at the moment. Can I help you?"

"Ah, yes, Mr. Thompson. I've read so much about your discoveries down at the lake lately. Quite amazing, really, and congratulations on your promotion to staff engineer at the Space Center. It must be hard going back and forth between the Space Center and Antarctica."

"Thank you. It's not too bad. We've made a few trips back and forth between home and Antarctica, but it looks like I'll be on-site at the lake for a while now to work on a few projects. What can I help you with, sir?"

"Oh, yes, Mr. Thompson, ah, we're at JPL using equipment similar to the equipment your father used at the Space Center when he discovered the lake in Antarctica," said the lead scientist. "We've been studying Jupiter's moon Europa with new thermal sensors that were sent to Europa on the Jupiter X explorer spacecraft."

"My dad told me you guys were studying a large sea recently discovered under the ice on Europa," Bud said.

"Yes, we were using the same supercomputer and software used to discover the lake there in Antarctica."

"That's cool. Did you want to leave a message for my dad?"

"Ah, yes, right. Please tell him we have discovered large amounts of silicon carbide with a chemical formula SiC in a group of mountains rising from the sea below the ice, and—"

Bud interrupted. "SiC?"

"Well, to make a long story short, we appear to have discovered a pocket of Europa's ocean surrounded by mountains with characteristics similar to the lake you discovered in Antarctica. In other words, it may have the same light source as the one that was discovered in your Antarctic lake, Mr. Thompson."

"Does that mean there is life under Europa's ice?" Bud asked.

"Well, we don't know at the moment, but that's why we need your father's help. Could you have him call us at JPL?"

"Sure thing, sir. Be glad to give him the message. Did you want to leave your name?"

"Just tell him his old friend from JPL. He'll know who. Oh, one more thing," said the lead scientist. "The temperature reading in the pocket of ocean surrounded by mountains under Europa's ice is 70 degrees Fahrenheit."

Bud raised his eyebrows. "Yes, sir, I'll let him know right away. I'm sure he will want to know more about your discovery. Thank you for calling."

Bud used the local communication system he and Peter had set up to connect to the lake, where his father was working. He tapped the screen on his cell phone.

"Thompson here," Bud's father said.

"Dad, you just received an important call from JPL," Bud said.

"Did they say what they wanted?"

"Well, remember that moon you told me about named Europa? They said they discovered a massive sea under the ice, and get this: part of it is surrounded with something called SiC in the mountains and has a water temperature of 70 degrees."

"I'm on my way back up to the camp," Bud's father said with urgency.

"Thought you might say that," replied Bud with a grin. Bud disconnected the line and sat back in his chair, looking at the large poster-sized image of Jupiter next to another large, poster-sized image labeled "Europa" on the wall.

Bud smiled big. "Life on Europa? I wonder ..."

THE END

DON'T MISS BUD THOMPSON'S NEXT EXCITING
ADVENTURE COMING SOON ...

BENEATH
THE
LAKE

Preview

— 1 —

"Bud! Bud Thompson! Mr. Thompson!" Ms. Crothers said as her voice increased in tone and volume with each attempt to get Bud's attention.

Peter kicked Bud's chair from the side.

Bud looked up from the wooden desk at Peter and suddenly realized the rest of the class was looking directly at him. Bud quickly tucked away the images of the Teko cave walls he had been working on under his text book. Ms. Crothers's voice was slowly starting to register.

"I, uh, um," Bud stammered as he tried to figure out what she had asked him. All eyes were on him as his distant classmates started to giggle while he continued to fumble. Bud could feel butterflies in his stomach bouncing around and trying to fly out.

"Now, Mr. Thompson, I know you spend much of your time these days down at the lake, but you must complete your course work," Ms. Crothers said with the entire class still watching Bud's every move. "Now please tell us, what is the chemical element that is the most abundant in the universe, but relatively rare on earth?"

Bud took a deep breath and thought about the tree house he designed. "Ah, yes, Ms. Crothers, that would be hydrogen, which is the chemical element with the atomic number 1. It is the lightest and most abundant element in the universe. While it is relatively rare on Earth in a natural state, it can easily be separated from the water molecule H_2O with electrolysis into two atoms of hydrogen and one atom of oxygen."

Ms. Crothers stared at Bud with her mouth open.

Bud continued with confidence, "For those who don't know what electrolysis is, it is simply the process in which an electrical current is passed through water, which frees the hydrogen and oxygen atoms from the water molecule. The camp uses the same process for its backup energy. And I use it to power up my tree house back home, where—"

"Ah, yes, thank you, Mr. Thompson. Very good," Ms. Crothers interrupted. She went back to her lecture. "As Mr. Thompson pointed out, chemistry is important in our daily lives …"

Bud sank down in his seat, retrieved the picture of the cave wall from under his book, and continued looking at it with curiosity.

"Nice, Bud. That was impressive, the way you spanked Ms. C," Peter whispered, shaking his head. "Jeez, did you have to get so intense?"

Bud just shrugged without looking up.

"… class dismissed," said Ms. Crothers. "Please don't forget to work on your homework. It is due first thing tomorrow morning." Ms. Crothers paused briefly as she looked through some papers and then continued, "Bud and Peter, may I have a word with you both?"

"Uh-oh," muttered Peter.

Bud walked to the front of the class, with Peter following closely behind him. All the other students quickly made their way out of the classroom before Ms. Crothers could call them to stay after, too.

Bud stood in front of Ms. Crothers and looked at her long, soft blonde hair flowing down to her waist. He blushed when Ms. Crothers caught him looking.

"Now, boys, I know you have a mission planned at the lake, but I do expect you to complete all your course work. Is that understood?"

"Yes, Ms. Crothers. No problem," Bud said, looking down.

"You can turn in your work once you come back from your mission, but please don't forget to complete it. Your grade for the year depends on it. Understood?"

Both the boys eagerly agreed.

"Boys, when your lake mission is over, I will be teaching an advanced renewable-energy class, and I want you both to participate in it. Can I sign you up for that?" she said as her voice changed from sharply harsh to more relaxed and kind now that the classroom was clear of other students. "I have already discussed it with your father, Bud, and Peter, I have talked with your father, too. However, I want to make sure you're both committed to it."

"Yes, Ms. Crothers. I'd like that," Bud said with a half smile, still looking down at his shoes.

"Me, too," Peter said.

"Good, then—off you go, now. I will see you when you get back. Your father says you have an important mission and will be spending time working with the Teko at the lake. Have a nice time, and please be safe."

"Yes, ma'am," Bud replied with a sideways grin as he looked at her quickly. He then noticed that Peter was still staring at her and hadn't moved.

"Peter," whispered Bud as he nudged his friend.

"Oh, yes, sorry. Yes, Ms. Crothers."

Bud grabbed Peter's arm and gave it a tug. They dashed out of the classroom.

Casey met them at the door and barked.

"Hey, Case," Bud said.

Casey looked up at Bud with bright eyes and barked again. It was hard to believe Casey was almost twelve years old now. He clearly looked like a two-year-old again.

"I saw you checking out Ms. Crothers," Bud said with a smirk.

"So?" replied Peter. "You did, too. Besides, Mr. Show-off, did you have to slam-dunk the hydrogen bit?"

"Aw, c'mon," Bud said, picking up the pace. "We need to get to the computer lab; my dad will be starting his speech in five minutes. We can watch him there."

BUD AND PETER SAT down in front of the large flat-panel display in the laboratory that had recently been set up for them. Casey was running in circles. He jumped onto Bud with a thud.

"Casey, please! Down. No. No," Bud said. He pushed the dog off his lap. "Man, he has so much energy these days."

"Looks like your dad is going to start," Peter said.

The live webcast had begun. Bud's father walked up a short set of stairs and onto the stage.

"Man, that's a large crowd at Berkeley," Peter remarked.

"It's the World Conference on Scientific Research and Exploration, after all," Bud said. "Looks like a whole bunch of people want to hear the plan for the mission to Jupiter's moon."

"Amazing to me that they found a warm sea under the ice on Europa," Peter said.

Bud's father calmly walked to the podium and set his notes down. The audience came to their feet, giving him a loud round of applause.

"Looks like they like your dad."

Bud smiled.

"Thank you. Thank you." The applause continued. Bud's father motioned for the crowd to sit. "Please, thank you. Please," he said, trying to get the crowd to take their seats.

The audience sat down at last and became quiet.

Bud's father cleared his throat. "Good morning. I am proud to be here today to give you an update on the mission to Europa. The incredible discoveries that have been made by the team at the Lake in Antarctica …"

Peter gave Bud a fist bump without turning away from the monitor. "That's us!" Peter said.

"Aww, yeah," Bud added.

"… have continued to change the way we think about evolution. Not only did we discover an entire civilization, complete with diverse life forms, that we would have never imagined, but we also discovered that blue, red, and white light can be generated by a combination of mineral and biological processes to enable vegetation to grow and evolve. We're still trying to fully understand how these systems work, and more important, how they have been able to evolve in concert with the evolution of mammals, reptiles, fish, bird, and insect life. In short, we discovered a world within our world …"

Bud was already getting bored. He had a number of projects to finish before they went down to the lake. Bud moved over to the workbench next to the computer screen and picked up where he had left off working on his latest robotic inventions. He attached an electronic component to the circuit board and picked up the hot soldering tool. He put the tool on the circuit board and melted the solder to secure the component into place. A column of smoke rolled off the solder.

"What's that thing, Bud?" Peter asked.

Bud continued soldering the electronic gizmo he was holding. "It's a robotic ant."

"Ant? What does it do?"

"It's pretty cool. I'm adding sensors that Larry sent me from the Space Center to a basic miniature robot. It will give us video, audio, basic temperatures—"

"You mean it will act sort of like a scout for us when we explore the caves?"

"*Exactamundo*," said Bud. "It even has sensors for oxygen, carbon monoxide, and hydrogen sulfide. Basically it will tell us if the air is good to breathe in the caves far beneath the lake. My dad asked Larry to make sure I added them."

"But I thought there was plenty of air in the caves?" asked Peter.

"Well, there may not be where we're going. We're going way beyond where the Teko live," Bud said. "Larry also gave us some gas masks to wear if the sensors detect any bad air in the caves … which of course I modified."

"Of course," Peter said, shaking his head.

"Check this out." Bud went to a storage closet and opened it up, pulling out four boxes with straps. They were about eighteen inches wide by two feet long by six inches in depth.

"What the heck are those? They look huge."

"Well, Larry sent me the basics, and I adapted them. Think of them as small power plants. I call them hydro-paks. Got to thinking. Since electrolysis produces hydrogen, we could use that to power flashlights in the caves we explore." Bud put one on the table and opened it up.

"It gets better," Bud continued. "What else does electrolysis do?"

"Got me. What?" Peter said, inspecting the device.

"Oxygen. Electrolysis also results in oxygen being produced. So there you have it: we fill the tank with water from the caves, and use it to power the lights and store oxygen and hydrogen."

"How you going to do the electrolysis? A battery or something?"

"Yep, there is a rechargeable battery. I had Larry send me some motion sensors. Each time we take a step, it will generate electricity and recharge the battery."

"Pretty cool," Peter said. "But what if we don't find water?"

"Yeah, I thought about that, too. Larry gave me a few methane power packs that will give us power for a couple of weeks if we need it."

"What the heck is methane?"

"Oh, ah … just think of it as the gas poop generates."

Peter just looked at Bud with a blank stare. "Really? Really, Bud? We're using poop to generate power now? That's gross!"

"Not our poop—yikes! Cow poop. But the methane is already refined into a liquid, so we just plug in a methane fuel cell into our lights if we need it. He gave me some extra fuel cells just in case. You know Larry—he always has backups."

"How the heck we going to carry all that stuff?" asked Peter.

"Glad you asked." Bud tapped on his cell phone.

Out burst an electronic robot from another storage cabinet, walking as if it were a pet dog. Casey started barking at it.

Peter jumped.

"Easy, Case. It's okay," Bud said as he controlled the robot.

"Holy cow! Where did you get that?"

"Well, a company built a robot called Big Dog. Larry contracted with that company to build a smaller version for us. He knew we would need to have something to carry our supplies."

"That's totally cool. It actually walks sort of like Casey," Peter said as he watched the robot move each mechanical leg.

Bud stopped it and started securing the hydro-paks onto it.

Peter pulled out his cell phone. "While we're doing show and tell, I wanted to show you what I just finished for the trip. It will help us map the caves. It is a GPS mapping tool."

Bud started laughing.

"What? Why are you laughing?"

"We can't get a GPS signal in the caves. What are you thinking?" Bud asked with a smirk.

"No kidding? Gee, I forgot," Peter said sarcastically, pushing Bud's shoulder. "I adapted the GPS app to track based on motion, sort of like your charger over there. So when we take a step, it tracks it. We'll each carry one, so it triangulates and tracks our path as we go. I just upload the data to my laptop and voilà—it builds a map of the caves." Peter showed Bud a test map on his computer.

"I take it back. This is cool," Bud said, looking closer at the cell phone.

"What about Little One?" Peter asked.

"Larry had NASA make a special face piece for him just in case we get into a cave that has no oxygen to breathe," Bud said. He took out eleven more of the miniature robots and placed them on the workbench.

Bud looked over at his father on the computer screen as he continued his speech. "… the support of an international scientific research fund established by the international monetary fund organization, NASA, JPL, and a long list of private companies and private donors, we're now ready to complete the final preparations for a mission to Jupiter's moon Europa, with the Europa One space vehicle and deep-sea probe, which will penetrate through miles of ice using a self-contained nuclear-powered heat probe to explore the solar system's largest body of water." The audience broke out in applause and came to their feet once again.

Sara pushed through the computer-room door in a rush. "Bud, we need to go," Sara said. "Little One is expecting us in thirty minutes. You need to finish packing and get moving."

"Okay, just watching Dad. I have everything I need in my backpack in our quarters. I just need to finish my ant army real quick, and then I'll go grab it and meet up with you at the transport." Bud pulled out an electronic device from a drawer on the workbench. "Here, give this to Tom. It's the latest version of our translator device. He needs to flash it with his latest software. Tell him to bring his laptop, too." Bud handed Sara what looked to be just another smart cell phone.

"Okay, but hurry. Peter, you need to get your stuff, too. I talked with your dad earlier today and told him Tom and I would be going to the lake with you and Bud," said Sara. Bud hardly recognized his sister's cheerful tone sometimes; she seemed very happy these days as long as Tom was close by.

Suddenly Sara saw the metal robot walking like Casey. "What the heck?"

"Cool, huh?" Bud said.

"What is it?"

"It's our supply carrier. But we need a name for it. Any ideas?"

"I don't know. Call it Robopooch or something."

"That's it. Robopooch it is." Casey barked at it again. Sara shook her head and walked out of the room.

Bud made some final adjustments to the robots and then piled them all into a small bag. He took off in a jog to get his backpack, with Casey keeping up stride for stride.

Rick Rowe is also the author of *Changing the World One Invention at a Time*. He lives in Las Vegas, Nevada, with his wife and two golden retrievers. To learn more about Rick and his upcoming projects, visit his website at www.rickrowe.com. You can also visit the website www.creaturesofthelake.com or visit the Facebook page.

9 781462 011278